IN THE LINE OF FIRE
EIGHT WOMEN WAR SPIES

Other Scholastic paperbacks you will enjoy:

Remember the Ladies
Norma Johnston

Sojourner Truth
Patricia C. McKissack and Fredrick McKissack

Standing Tall
Argentina Palacios

Nelson Mandela, "No Easy Walk to Freedom"
Barry Denenberg

IN THE LINE OF FIRE
EIGHT WOMEN WAR SPIES

GEORGE SULLIVAN

SCHOLASTIC INC.
New York Toronto London Auckland Sydney

ISBN 0-590-48294-7

Copyright © 1996 by George Sullivan.
All rights reserved. Published by Scholastic Inc.

12 11 10 9 8 7 6 5 4 3 2 1   6 7 8 9/9 0 1/0

Printed in the U.S.A.   40

First Scholastic printing, March 1996

Acknowledgments

A great many people helped the author by providing background information, photographs, or other pieces of artwork that were used in this book. Special thanks are due the following: S. Katherine Schneider, Gerald Haines, and Lynda McCarthy, Central Intelligence Agency; Maja Keech, Prints and Photographs Division, Library of Congress; John Taylor, James G. Cassedy, and Kenneth D. Schlessinger, National Archives; Robert A. Harman, Janice Dockery, and Louise Jones, The Historical Society of Philadelphia; Keith Hughes, *Smithsonian* Magazine; Carolyn Cole, Los Angeles Public Library; Claude Jackson and Stephen Massengill, North Carolina Department of Cultural Resources; Merle Chamberlain, Lower Cape Fear Historical Society Archives; Beverly Tetterton, New Hanover (North Carolina) Public Library; Andy Kraushaar, State Historical Society of Wisconsin; Dave Johnson and John Curry, Michigan State Archives; Geoffrey A. White, Hawaii State Archives; James Lowe and Sal Alberti, James Lowe Autographs; Francesca Kurti, TLC Labs; Elizabeth McIntosh, Tom Harris, Joseph Fricelli, and Don Wigal.

Contents

Introduction

Spying is not a nice profession. The business of snooping on one's enemies — or friends — seldom earns praise.

The Central Intelligence Agency (CIA), the government agency that collects information by secret means on more than 150 nations, never uses the word "spy." Its spies are called operatives, officers, or agents. (The CIA doesn't like the word "secret" either; it prefers "classified.")

Despite its kind of scrubby reputation, there's always been great fascination with spying. Spies enjoy the thrills and excitement of being criminals, while maintaining the identity of honest citizens. A spy can lie, cheat, and steal — without ever being considered an evildoer.

Every country has its own intelligence-gathering network and almost all nations of the world spy

1

on one another (while denying they do so). The use of spies by America's military leaders is as old as the nation itself, even older. During the Revolutionary War, General George Washington sent scores of agents behind the battle lines to collect intelligence about the British.

In those days, an agent could be almost anyone with the courage and determination the job requires. Farmers, traveling merchants and craftsmen, and country women seeking to purchase food for their families, any and all of whom could pass back and forth through enemy lines without arousing suspicion were sought by Washington to seek out scraps of information.

In official reports, Washington made no mention of women employed as spies. Even Lydia Darragh, whose heroics in gathering information about enemy troops has been well documented, received no recognition. It may be that Washington did not want to reveal the names of secret agents, male or female, for fear it could be hazardous to their health.

During the Civil War, the era of amateur spying continued. Both the Union and the Confederacy recruited agents from every segment of society. They made spies of physicians and peddlers, housewives and servants. Countless slaves were used as couriers, carrying secret dispatches to military leaders.

Women were in great demand as spies during the Civil War because they seldom came under suspicion and, if caught, were rarely handed harsh sentences.

In 1942, the year following the attack on Pearl Harbor, the United States got into the intelligence-gathering business in a serious way with the founding of the Office of Strategic Services (OSS) by Major General William J. Donovan. During World War II, the OSS sent hundreds of agents and guerilla fighters into a dozen enemy-occupied nations in Europe and Asia.

About 20 percent of the approximately 26,000 people who worked for the OSS were women, most of whom were assigned to desk jobs at the agency's Washington headquarters. Many of them dealt with secret reports and coded and decoded messages. Some were specially trained in code-breaking and map-making.

While only a small percentage of OSS women ever went overseas, and fewer still were assigned to operational jobs behind enemy lines, several had extraordinary careers. One was Virginia Hall, the daughter of a prominent Baltimore family. An agent in German-occupied France, Hall organized guerilla units, arranged parachute drops of weapons, and kept in contact with her OSS superiors by means of a secret radio transmitter. After the war, Hall received the Distinguished Service Cross for heroism. Never before had the medal been given to a woman.

After World War II, the OSS was disbanded. But in the postwar years, with the United States in conflict with the Soviet Union in the Cold War, the nation's need for intelligence about the Soviets became obvious. Out of that need came the CIA, which was founded in 1947.

The twentieth century has been called the century of the spy. And no wonder. At one time, the intelligence-gathering agencies of the Soviet Union, principally the KGB, employed more than 200,000 men and women. To oppose this throng, the CIA recuited an army of men and women almost as big. (The exact number of CIA employees is classified.)

After the Soviet Union broke up in 1991 and the Cold War ended, the KGB was taken apart. But spying continues. Russia today has four intelligence-gathering agencies and maintains fully staffed "residences" in their many embassies and consulates.

Great Britain is the only other nation of the world to operate a spy network that is on a par with those of the United States and Russia. The British, in fact, have two agencies: M.I.6 — the Intelligence Bureau of the Foreign Office — sends spies into foreign countries; M.I.5 is responsible for counter espionage and also wars against terrorism.

In 1992, the British startled the world of spying by naming Stella Rimington, a woman in her late fifties, as chief of M.I.5. She was the first woman to head one of Britain's secret agencies.

Within the first two years of her appointment, Rimington achieved other firsts. She became the first director to hold a televised news conference and she was the first person from the world of espionage to have her photograph appear in the pages of a gossip magazine. (The photograph was featured in *Hello!*, a weekly magazine published in Great Britain that is filled with celebrity photos and chitchat.)

Stella Rimington is unique. The truth is that for decades the world's most famous spymasters distrusted women espionage agents and even feared them. The Soviet Union's Richard Sorge, one of the most brilliant spies of recent times, described women as "unfit for espionage work."

Within the CIA and other intelligence agencies, few women had positions of authority. They were handed jobs in office management; they did research and analysis. "There was a feeling that women weren't as stable as men in critical situations," says a retired CIA field officer.

In the past couple of decades or so, that situation has begun to change. William E. Colby, director of the CIA from 1973–1976, who supported the equality of women in government, helped to pioneer the change. Colby foresaw the day when a woman would be appointed director of the CIA.

Colby said that women have a greater "sense of humanity" than men. Truly successful women, he said, use the power of their minds, not pressure, to influence people.

While, through the years, there may not have been a great number of women spies as compared to men, there have been some truly fascinating ones. This book tells of some of them.

5

1
The Spy Who Saved George Washington

During the American Revolution, the world's most powerful nation, Great Britain, faced a small ragtag army under the command of General George Washington. Because the patriots were regularly outmanned and outgunned, Washington sometimes used such unheard-of tactics as having his troops disguise themselves in British uniforms and attack from the rear. He also allowed false documents to fall into British hands and even had fake military facilities built.

Besides relying on deception, Washington was highly skilled in collecting intelligence, and obtained a "secret service fund" from the Continental Congress for that purpose. Washington had travelers questioned for any information that might be useful, and he sent forth dozens of agents on intelligence-gathering missions.

Lydia Darragh became a key figure in Washington's intelligence network in 1777, the year British General William Howe marched into Philadelphia. The Continental Congress, which had been meeting in the city, was forced to flee.

Philadelphia was where the Declaration of Independence had been written, one reason the British referred to the city as the place where all the "trouble" started. It must have given King George III special pleasure to know that the British flag was flying over Independence Hall.

While the British were getting settled in Philadelphia, Washington rested his army of some 11,000 men at Perkiomen Creek for a few days before establishing a more permanent camp at Whitemarsh, close to Norristown, about 12 miles northwest of Philadelphia.

Despite the recent setbacks, and the fact that his soldiers lacked proper food and clothing, General Washington remained hopeful. He even went so far as to ask his generals whether they would recommend a winter campaign, the goal of which would be to drive the British out of Philadelphia. However, there was little, if any, support for the idea. The Marquis de Lafayette seemed to voice what most of Washington's staff members were thinking when he recommended that the general give the men "a good rest in winter quarters."

While Washington and his army sought to cope with the bitter cold and drifting snow at Whitemarsh, the British were experiencing the warm comforts of life in Philadelphia. Their willingness to enjoy themselves caused Benjamin Franklin to remark that "Howe had not taken Philadelphia, but Philadelphia had taken Howe."

When the British had taken over the city, the officers seized the best houses for themselves. General Howe, for example, used the residence of Captain John Cadwalader, a dedicated patriot, as his headquarters. Directly opposite the Cadwalader dwelling, at 177 South Second Street, was Loxley House, the comfortable house of William and Lydia Darragh, who were members of the Society of Friends, or Quakers, and as such, were deeply opposed to war. General Howe chose the Darragh home for its spacious parlor, which would serve as a conference room for British officers.

Several times that fall groups of red-coated British officers assembled in the Darragh parlor and, by candlelight, discussed plans for upcoming campaigns. The meetings deeply offended Lydia and her husband but they knew they were powerless to prevent them.

During the final weeks of November 1777, Lydia noticed that the British officers suddenly became more serious. They spent less time seeking the pleasures of the city and more time drilling the soldiers under their command.

George Washington was also aware of the change that had taken place. When Philadelphia had fallen to the British after the defeat at Brandywine, Washington had assigned Colonel Elias Boudinot, a noted patriot and statesman, to set up listening posts at several points on the outskirts of Philadelphia. Boudinot's agents were ordinary men and women who were able to enter the enemy-held city without causing any concern, and return with pieces of military information. They were merchants, farmers, artisans, and country girls selling eggs, cheese, and other farm products. They sought to obtain information concerning the arrival or departure of troops, the movement of weapons or heavy equipment, changes in heavy-gun emplacements, and the stockpiling of equipment and supplies.

Boudinot met his agents at the Rising Sun Tavern, near Frankford, several miles north of Philadelphia. Afterward, he would put together all the bits and pieces to form a picture of what was happening. By the last days of November, it had become obvious that the British were "in motion." The troops were being equipped and supplied for a major undertaking.

Where and when was it going to take place? Boudinot could only guess.

When the news of how active the British had become was passed on to Washington, he took it very seriously, and called for reinforcements. Some 1,200 Rhode Island troops and 1,000 more from Virginia, Maryland, and Pennsylvania were ordered to join his army at Whitemarsh. Washington could then only wait until he received more news about the enemy's plans.

Washington could never have guessed the information he was waiting for would be furnished by so unlikely a source as Lydia Darragh. No one would ever have taken her for a spy. She was a sweet-faced woman, always polite and considerate, who dressed in an ankle-length skirt of gray muslin and a bonnet with a large brim that framed her face.

In her dealings with British officers, Lydia made no secret of the fact that she and her husband supported the Colonial cause. In fact, the British admired her for her spirit.

When Lydia expressed her feelings about the war, she never sounded hostile. "We detest the sin while pitying the sinner," she told one officer, expressing her Quaker beliefs. "Though we consider thee as a public enemy, we regard thee as a private friend. While we detest the cause thee fights for, we wish well to thy personal interest and safety."

The British would have been surprised to learn that for several weeks Lydia had been sending bits of information about what was going on in the city to her oldest son, Lieutenant Charles Darragh, a member of Washington's army at Whitemarsh. She used her youngest son, John, who was 14, as a courier. She felt he was so young and innocent-looking that he would never be suspected.

Lydia's career as an undercover agent was about to mushroom. On the afternoon of December 2, a British officer called upon Lydia at her home. "We will require the use of the parlor at eight o'clock this evening," he said. Lydia nodded in agreement. Then the officer suggested that the family retire early, "as we wish to use the room without interruption."

This was an unusual request and it made Lydia suspicious.

The officers began arriving promptly at eight o'clock. Lydia was there to greet them and take their hats and coats. She noticed they were all officers of high rank. This was obviously a very important meeting.

After the last officer arrived, Lydia locked the front door and went upstairs to her bedroom, where her husband was already sound asleep. But Lydia could not sleep. It always disturbed her when the British used her home, but tonight she was much more uneasy than usual. What was the purpose of this mysterious conference? As she lay in her bed, she listened intently for voices from the parlor, but she could hear nothing.

Finally, Lydia couldn't stand it any longer. She threw back the covers, gathered a dressing gown about her shoulders and, in stockinged feet, tiptoed out into the hall and down the unlighted stairway. She crossed the hallway and listened from behind the parlor's closed, paneled door.

The officers were talking quietly. One told of information he had just received. This news confirmed reports that Washington's army was now encamped at Whitemarsh in "unprepared condition." When the officer had finished speaking, other officers recited the strength of their own units, giving the numbers of troops and types of equipment each had available.

Then Lydia heard the voice of still another officer. He spoke slowly and distinctly but in tones so low that she could not make out what he was saying. Then it dawned on her that he must be dictating an order to someone seated beside him who was taking down his words with a quill pen. Lydia pressed her ear to the door but still could not hear. Then the room fell silent.

Suddenly a clear voice started reading aloud. Lydia heard an order for the British troops to march out of Philadelphia on the night of December 4 to launch an attack on General Washington's army. Taken by surprise by a superior force, the patriot army would be destroyed.

Lydia had heard all she wanted to hear. She hurried back to her room and went to bed, her heart pounding. Over and over in her mind she kept repeating the words she had just heard, that there was to be a surprise attack on General Washington's army in two days. Lydia knew the news must be carried to Washington — but how?

Her mind was filled with such thoughts when she heard footsteps in the hallway outside her bedroom and then a soft knock on the door. Lydia did not move.

Then the knock was repeated, this time more firmly. Still, Lydia did not move.

When the knock came a third time, it was even louder than before. "Mrs. Darragh?" she heard a voice call out . . . and more knocking.

Lydia pretended she had been awakened. In what she hoped sounded like a sleepy voice, she called out, "Just a moment, sir."

When she finally went to the door, Lydia acted

as if she were not yet fully awake. The officer standing before her apologized for disturbing her and explained the meeting was over and the officers were leaving. He asked her to blow out the remaining candles and douse any coals still glowing on the grate.

Afterward, Lydia got undressed and went to bed. But it was almost daylight before she was able to fall asleep.

In the morning as she was getting dressed, Lydia decided that she and she alone must get the information to General Washington. By the time she was ready to go downstairs for breakfast, she knew exactly how she would do it.

At breakfast, Lydia announced, "What a pity, we are out of flour. I will have to go to Frankford and get some from the mill."

A frown crossed her husband's face. "Send one of the servants," he said. "There is no good reason that thee should make such a long trip."

"No," said Lydia firmly. "I shall go myself."

"But at least take one of the maids with thee," her husband said.

"I shall go alone," Lydia said. From the way she said it, her husband realized that it would make no sense to further discuss the matter.

The Frankford flour mill, about five miles northeast of the city, was on the road to Whitemarsh. Women of Philadelphia made the trip to the mill frequently. Before setting out, Lydia had to stop at General Howe's headquarters and acquire a pass that would allow her to get through British lines. She was able to do this easily since her house was used as a meeting place for British officers.

Once she had the pass, Lydia hurried through the streets of Philadelphia. When she reached the outskirts of the city, she was halted by British sentries. She showed them her pass and explained her mission, showing them the empty flour bag she carried, and was allowed to continue her journey.

On the road to Frankford, the winter wind swept across bleak fields and Lydia drew her cloak tightly about her neck. She walked so fast she almost ran.

When Lydia reached the mill, it was early in the afternoon. She rested for a short while, then gave her sack to the miller and told him she was going down the road to visit friends. "I'll be back soon," she said.

Lydia then set out for Whitemarsh. She was beginning to get weary and footsore but she hurried on, fired by her fierce determination to warn Washington.

She had traveled two or three miles beyond the mill when she saw in the distance an American officer on horseback. With him were several soldiers, members of a scouting party. They had been sent out by Washington to watch the roads and gather information about the British. Little did they suspect what they were about to hear.

As the officer drew closer, Lydia recognized him, and waved. It was Lieutenant Colonel Thomas Craig, a family friend.

"What are you doing here, Lydia," Craig asked, "and how did you get through the British lines?"

As the lieutenant colonel was dismounting, Lydia explained she had come to get flour at the Frankford mill. "General Howe gave me a pass," she said.

"But you are far beyond Frankford," Craig said.

"I know," said Lydia, and then began to tell all she had overheard the night before.

"Tomorrow, December fourth," Lydia said, "the British are to leave Philadelphia at dawn for Whitemarsh." She also gave him many details of the attack, including the information that General Howe would be leaving the city with 5,999 men, 13 pieces of cannon, baggage wagons, and 11 boats on wagon wheels (an early form of amphibious military vehicle).

The young lieutenant colonel was astounded by what Lydia had told him.

"Should I take you to the general?" he asked.

"No," said Lydia. "It is enough for you to know. It should be your duty to tell him. But you must agree not to reveal the source of your information. If it became known, I might pay with my life."

"It shall be as you wish," he said. "But first you must rest and have food."

Lydia protested. She was eager to return to Philadelphia as quickly as possible.

The lieutenant colonel insisted, and before riding off he escorted Lydia to a nearby farmhouse where she had a light meal before setting out on her return journey. She remembered to stop at the mill at Frankford to get her sack of flour. When she finally reached home, she was on the brink of exhaustion. But she had a sense of well-being, confident that she had done the right thing.

Well before dawn the next morning, Lydia was awakened by the beating of drums and the tramp of marching feet. From her bedroom window, she looked out to see columns of British soldiers marching out of Philadelphia. She prayed that Washington had received her message and all would go well for the general and his men.

The British arrived at Chestnut Hill not long after daybreak and dug into positions along a ridge there. To their surprise, they found the Pennsylvania militia waiting for them. Instead of retreating, as the British had been expecting, several American companies dashed forward and began firing at them.

General Howe passed the day probing the American positions, looking for soft spots. But he found none. When darkness fell, he changed his ground, moving to a hill on the Americans' left flank, about a mile from Washington's camp. When General Howe sent out scouting parties to test the American strength, he again found the Colonial troops solidly entrenched, as immovable as a stone wall.

The next day and the day after brought more of the same. Small parties of British troops ventured forward to test the Colonials, then fell back. There was no major engagement.

On the morning of December 8, the Colonials noticed sudden activity in the British camp. Long strings of fires had been lit. At first, the Americans thought the British were planning to launch an

16

attack. But before long they realized the redcoats were retreating to Philadelphia and the fires were meant to cover their departure.

Washington sent several squads of soldiers to pursue the departing British, and no doubt would have liked to have attacked them with a major force. But the condition of his men prevented him from doing so. In a report to Congress, Washington wrote:

> *I sincerely wish that they had made an attack, as the issue in all probability, from the disposition of our troops and the strong situation of our camp, would have been fortunate and happy. At the same time, I must add, that reason, prudence, and every principle of policy, forbade us from quitting our post to attack them.*

On the night after the return of the redcoats, the British officer who had arranged the meeting at Lydia's home called upon her. After they had seated themselves in the parlor, he said, "What I wish to know is whether any of your family was up on the night that I met with other officers in this house."

Lydia shook her head. "No," she said in a gentle voice. "They all retired early. This was as you ordered."

The officer looked at her firmly. "I know you were asleep," he said, "because I had to knock at your chamber door three times before you heard me. But I wonder whether anyone else was about?"

"Why?"

"Because someone must have given General Washington information about our plans. When we reached Whitemarsh, we found their cannon mounted and their soldiers ready to receive us. The result was we wasted days marching out and back, without ever injuring the enemy, and returning here like a pack of fools."

Lydia Darragh offered her sympathy.

A few days later, General Washington led his soldiers out of Whitemarsh to Valley Forge, where he established winter quarters. Located on high ground along the west bank of the Schuylkill River about 22 miles northwest of Philadelphia, Valley Forge offered a commanding view of strategic roads and the potential to become a defensive stronghold.

Some historical accounts of this period credit Lydia Darragh with saving General Washington's army from destruction. But Washington never mentioned Lydia in any of his reports or journals. Neither was her achievement ever officially recognized by any of the other leaders of the Colonial cause. Lydia had to be content with the satisfaction that comes from knowing she had risen to the demands of the moment and in so doing had made an important contribution to the successful struggle for American independence and freedom.

2
Rebel Rose

During the Civil War, Rose O'Neal Greenhow (or Rebel Rose as Northerners called her) was, for a time, the Confederacy's most active and dedicated spy. Wellborn and rich, a woman of unusual grace and intelligence, Mrs. Greenhow risked death in her desire to help the Confederate cause. It was Southern women such as Mrs. Greenhow that the Wilmington *Messenger* newspaper must have had in mind when it observed: "The men are as brave as lions and the women are as brave as the men."

Rose Greenhow lived two lives. To her friends and acquaintances, she was a charming woman of fashion who entertained frequently. The other Rose Greenhow was a woman in a dark cloak who carried messages to aid the Southern cause. Deeply involved in the Civil War from its first battle, she did not live to see its end.

As young girls, Rose O'Neal and her sister, Ellen, were sent from Maryland to live with an aunt in Washington. The aunt ran a boardinghouse, renting rooms to congressmen and other government officials. In the years they were growing up, the O'Neal sisters came to know virtually everyone of importance in the various branches of government.

Among their aunt's boarders was John C. Calhoun, the great Southern statesman, a former secretary of state and vice president, who was elected to the Senate in 1832. Young Rose often listened to the old warrior as he spoke his mind about the political and social problems of the day.

In 1835, Rose married Robert Greenhow, a close friend of Calhoun's, who came from a distinguished Virginia family. A scholar, doctor, and author, Greenhow also served in the State Department for twenty-two years. He died in 1854.

The widowed Rose lived in a two-story brick home at the corner of Thirteenth and I streets in Washington, a fashionable part of the city. James Buchanan, the only bachelor president in the nation's history, who held office before Lincoln was elected in 1860, was a frequent visitor. So was Senator William Seward of New York, who was to serve Lincoln as his secretary of state.

Another important visitor to the Greenhow home was Massachusetts Senator Henry Wilson, chairman of the Senate Committee on Military Affairs. Wilson, fiftyish, portly and balding, found Rose impossible to resist.

When the Civil War erupted in 1861, Rose, who ardently supported the Southern cause, did not try to hide her feelings. Since Washington was much more a Southern city than a Northern one and was overflowing with men and women sympathetic to the Confederacy, people were quick to accept Rose's political stance.

While Rose was deeply loyal to the South, the thought of serving the Confederacy as a spy and betraying the trust of her many friends in high places probably never entered her mind. But then one day in May 1861, a friend, Thomas Jordan, came to call. Jordan at the time was a captain in the United States Army. But he explained to Rose that he was planning to resign his commission and join the Confederate Army to serve on General Beauregard's staff.

They discussed the war and the subject of loyalty. Rose said she wished she could do something to aid the Southern cause. "I am a Southern woman," she later was to write, "born with revolutionary blood in my veins."

Jordan suggested a way that Rose could help. He was organizing civilians who were in a position to contribute information that could be helpful to the South. Would Rose want to be included? She jumped at the chance, promising to pass on to Jordan anything of importance she might hear from her Washington friends. Before leaving, Jordan instructed Rose in the art of transmitting messages in code. Years later, Rose wrote of her decision to help Jordan: "To this end, I employed every capacity with which God endowed me, and the results were far more successful than my hopes could have flattered me to believe."

Rose's first dispatches were extremely valuable. They concerned the Battle of Bull Run, also called Manassas, the very first engagement of the war, fought only 30 miles from Washington.

In the early days of the conflict, neither side was really prepared to fight. Armies were poorly equipped, ill-trained, and scarcely even disciplined. The first battles were little more than frantic struggles between armed mobs.

So it was at Bull Run. Union forces were commanded by General Irvin McDowell, a willing but inexperienced leader. His "main Union Army" was made up of some 25,000 ragtag recruits who had rushed from every part of the North to aid in the defense of Washington. McDowell realized his untrained troops were not ready to fight, but Abraham Lincoln, under public pressure to produce a victory, ordered McDowell into battle. The general had no choice but to obey.

McDowell's initial plan was to march for two days into the central part of Virginia, known as the Piedmont, and capture Manassas Junction, an important railroad center. Confederate General Pierre G. T. Beauregard, who commanded approximately 25,000 troops, was expecting McDowell to make such a move. While Beauregard had a good idea where the Union forces were going to strike, he didn't know when. That information was provided by Rose Greenhow.

On July 10, Beauregard received from a courier a package the size of a silver dollar, which had been sewn into a black silk pouch. It contained a one-sentence message: "McDowell has been ordered to advance on the sixteenth." It was signed "R.O.G."

Beauregard reacted by placing his troops along the south bank of the shallow, meandering creek known as Bull Run, just north of Manassas. A second Confederate force of 12,000 troops was at Winchester, about 50 miles to the northwest. This army was under the command of General Joseph E. Johnston.

As the date of the impending battle drew near, General Beauregard wanted an up-to-date report on the situation. He secretly ferried a messenger across the Potomac River with orders to call upon Rose at her Washington home. Rose answered Beauregard's request with a hurriedly written note that confirmed the content of her first message. When the dispatch reached Beauregard, he telegraphed headquarters to request that General Johnston's 12,000 troops join his own army as reinforcements.

The next day, Rose received a reply from Thomas Jordan. It read: "Yours was received at eight o'clock at night. Let them come; we are ready for them. We rely on you for precise information. Be particular as to description and destination of forces, quantity of artillery, etc."

Rose wasted no time. The same day, she sent another message to Beauregard cautioning him that McDowell's army planned to destroy the railway line between Manassas and Winchester to prevent the arrival of Johnston's troops. Because of Rose's warning, Beauregard was able to keep McDowell's army in check. Most of Johnston's men joined Beauregard at Manassas on the eve of the battle.

On July 21, a sweltering Sunday, McDowell's troops attacked, seeking to pierce the left side of Beauregard's line. But they could not. Then the Southerners charged into McDowell's attacking troops, sending the Northerners reeling backward. As the Southern forces pressed their advantage, McDowell's raw recruits panicked and fled. What had been foreseen as a Northern victory ended in rout, with McDowell's men hobbling back toward Washington. The North was shocked by what happened at Manassas, while the South's confidence was given a sharp boost.

Afterward, Rose received another message from Jordan. It read: "Our President and our General direct me to thank you. We rely on you for further information. The Confederacy owes you a debt."

After Bull Run, Rose put aside her espionage activities briefly to attend to family business. She left Washington to travel to New York to put her second-oldest daughter, Leila, on a ship bound for California, where she was to join her older sister. Rose's youngest daughter, eight-year-old "Little Rose," remained with her mother.

Before the end of July, Rose was back in Washington. She began meeting with the band of spies that had been organized by Thomas Jordan. These men and women included Colonel Michael Thompson (who called himself Colonel Empty, a code name based on the speech sounds of his initials); Dr. Arran Van Camp, a dentist; and Lewis Linn McArthur, an Army clerk. Betty Duvall, Bettie Hassler, Lily Mackall, and George Donellan served as loyal couriers.

Rose's home was often used as a meeting place. She and her colleagues kept dispatches flowing to the Confederate capital at Richmond, detailing information about Union defenses in Washington. Rose also dispatched any tidbits of gossip she happened to hear.

Ordinarily, agents involved in undercover work try to keep a very low profile. By doing otherwise, they risk breaking the first commandment of spying, "Thou Shalt Not Get Caught." Rose Greenhow saw things differently. She moved openly and boldly through the capital on her information-gathering missions, confident that her well-placed friends would protect her. She even took to boasting about her accomplishments. Little wonder that federal officials ordered that she be put under close watch.

The person chosen to watch Rose was Allan J. Pinkerton, the nation's first private detective, who had been summoned to Washington to set up a federal secret service. Pinkerton's first move was to put Rose's home under surveillance. Arriving with two men as darkness was falling, Pinkerton saw light coming from between the slats of the closed blinds. The windows were too high for Pinkerton to look inside, so after pulling off his boots he climbed up on the shoulders of his two men. Inside he saw a visitor seated in the living room. A tall handsome man, about 40 years old, he was wearing the blue uniform of the Union Army. From the insignia, Pinkerton could tell he was an infantry captain.

In a few moments, Rose entered the room. The two sat at a table at the rear of the room and began to converse in low tones. Pinkerton strained to hear what they were saying but could not. The officer took a map out of his jacket pocket, held it up to the light, and he and Rose began discussing it. Pinkerton thought it looked like a plan of the fortifications in and around Washington.

Whenever a passerby approached, Pinkerton would jump to the ground and he and his two men would hide under the front staircase of Rose's house. On one such occasion, they heard the captain's footsteps on the front steps above them. He whispered good night, and then Pinkerton and his men heard what sounded like a kiss. The door closed and the captain descended the staircase. Pinkerton followed him along the dark streets. At the corner of Pennsylvania Avenue and F streets, the captain passed a posted sentry and darted into a building.

Pinkerton was trying to decide whether or not to follow, when suddenly four armed soldiers rushed out of the building and pointed their rifles at him. One shouted out, "Halt, or I fire."

Pinkerton realized he could not resist four armed men. He tried to explain his way out of the situation, saying he was a stranger in the city and had lost his way in the darkness, but his captors scarcely listened. He was taken upstairs to the office of the man he had been following.

"What is your name?" the captain demanded.

"E. J. Allen," said Pinkerton, calling upon an alias he often used.

"What is your business?"

"I have nothing further to say and I decline to answer further questions."

At that, the captain ordered Pinkerton to be taken downstairs to a cell occupied by several common criminals. During the night, Pinkerton persuaded one of the guards to deliver a message from him to Assistant Secretary of War Thomas A. Scott. Orders came the next morning to release Pinkerton and send him to Scott's home. Once there, Pinkerton explained all that he had seen and heard the night before.

"Mrs. Greenhow," Scott declared, "is becoming a dangerous character. You will therefore maintain your watch upon her. Should she be detected attempting to convey any information outside of the Union, she must be arrested at once."

Then Scott ordered that the captain whom Pinkerton had followed be brought to his house for questioning. It was quickly established that he was lying about his association with persons who were known to be disloyal to the Union. He was placed under arrest. In a search of the captain's house, soldiers found more incriminating evidence. The captain — whom Pinkerton referred to as "Ellison" — was imprisoned at Fort McHenry for more than a year. He died soon after his release.

Pinkerton and his men went back to watching Rose's house. A steady stream of prominent men poured in and out, including congressmen and senators. One man, an attorney, appeared virtually every night. Pinkerton decided he would shadow him. When he saw the attorney hand information to a courier, Pinkerton arrested him.

Eight days later, Rose herself was arrested. She was confronted by Pinkerton and one of his men as she mounted the front stairs of her home.

"Is this Mrs. Greenhow?" Pinkerton asked.

"Yes. Who are you and what do you want?"

"I have come to arrest you."

"By what authority?" she asked.

"By sufficient authority."

Then Rose demanded that Pinkerton show her the warrant for her arrest. Pinkerton could only explain that he had verbal authority from the Department of War and the State Department.

"I have no power to resist you," Rose said. "But had I been inside of my house, I would have killed you before I submitted to this illegal process."

Soon, Rose's house was filled with detectives searching drawers, closets, and bookcases for evidence. Little Rose, Rose's eight-year-old daughter, climbed a tree in the garden and shouted to the neighborhood, "Mama has been arrested!" Pinkerton's detectives climbed up the tree and brought her down.

Rose was not put in jail but confined to her home, where she was kept under constant watch. One of Pinkerton's agents even sat by her bed at night. Such treatment horrified her. A letter she wrote to friends in South Carolina was quoted by Mary Chesnut, the noted diarist.

She wants us to know how her delicacy was shocked and outraged. For eight days she was in the full sight of men, her rooms wide open, and sleepless sentinels watching by day and night. Soldiers tramping, looking at her leisurely by way of amusement.

In the weeks that followed, Union officials began to house other female prisoners in Fort Greenhow, as Rose's home came to be called. Pinkerton's detectives were replaced by troops from General McClellan's personal bodyguard, known as the Sturgis Rifles.

Other women who were known to support the Southern cause were also confined in the house. But Rose had little to do with any of them. She realized that one or more of them might be counterspies, planted to get incriminating evidence from her. Rose's only companion, aside from her daughter, was Mrs. Philip Phillips, who was being held at Fort Greenhow along with her two daughters and a sister.

Although Rose was watched, searched, and spied upon, she still managed to transmit news and gossip to Richmond. She took up needlepoint embroidery to keep herself occupied, and is believed to have woven color-coded messages into her tapestry work. She also later admitted that she used her small daughter as a courier, tucking messages into the soles of her shoes. When her captors began to realize that Little Rose had taken on the role of a messenger, she was not permitted to leave the house. By one means or another, a Richmond newspaper received a copy of a letter that Rose had sent to Secretary Seward complaining of her treatment. The newspaper promptly published it.

Rose wrote long, rambling poems that she sent to her friends. These were carefully studied for hidden meanings and coded messages. Early in January 1862, Major General John E. Wool telegraphed Secretary Seward to tell him that someone in Washington was supplying Confederate forces with detailed information about Union troops positions. "They know much better than I what is doing in Washington," Wool complained.

Fort Greenhow was eventually closed and Rose was transferred to Old Capitol Prison in Washington. Shabby and filthy, Old Capitol Prison was filled with captured rebel soldiers, suspected spies, Union Army deserters, and "contrabands," that is, escaped slaves who had no means of supporting themselves and who had been sent to prison as an act of "charity." Rose was assigned to a large room on the first floor that housed some twenty prisoners. Each had a bunk and little else. Rose's health suffered and she began losing weight.

Little Rose remained with her. "My little darling," she said to her daughter, "you must show yourself superior to these Yankees, and not pine."

"Oh, Mamma, never fear," the little girl replied. "I hate them too much."

When Little Rose became ill, her mother refused to allow her to be treated by the prison doctor. "At your peril, you touch my child," she declared. "You are a coward and not a gentleman, and an insult to women." Rose sent for her private doctor.

In March 1862, Rose was given a hearing in the office of the acting military governor. Judge Edward Pierrepont read the charges of espionage that had been brought against her. When he had finished, Rose said, "If I gave the information that you say I have, I must have got it from sources that were in the confidence of the government. If Mr. Lincoln's friends will pour into my ear such important information, am I to be held responsible for all that?"

Judge Pierrepont must have found it difficult to argue with Rose's reasoning, for he suggested that her misdeeds were perhaps more "mischief" than treason. Rose showed no gratitude for this opinion. Instead, she looked coldly at the judge and said, "In these war times, you ought to be in some more important business than holding an inquisition for the examination of women."

Judge Pierrepont decided to "parole" Rose and return her to the South, so she could no longer spy upon the North. She was transported through Union lines into Virginia in exchange for her promise not to return to the North for the duration of the war.

In Richmond, Rose was greeted as a heroine by most people, although some suspected she might be in the service of the Union as a counterspy. Before the end of the year, Rose sailed for Europe to help build support for the Confederacy. By this time, she had completed work on a book about her experiences. Titled *My Imprisonment and the First Year of Abolition Rule in Washington*, the book was published in London, and sold very well.

Little else is known about Rose's stay in Europe. She was a favorite of English society and became romantically involved with Lord Granville, to whom she became engaged.

Then in August 1864, Rose suddenly decided to leave her new circle of friends, her fiancé, and her daughter Rose, who was attending a convent school in Paris, and return to the South. Some sources say that Rose had been assigned to carry an important message to Jefferson Davis, president of the Confederacy, concerning England's entry into the war as a Confederate ally.

In any event, it was to be a quick trip. After a short stay, Rose planned to return, marry Granville, and live in England.

The Union Navy had blockaded Southern ports, but Rose booked passage on the *Condor*, which was a blockade runner, or light, low-lying ship capable of generating the short bursts of speed necessary to dash through the ring of blockaders. The *Condor's* destination was Wilmington, North Carolina.

A violent storm engulfed the ship as it neared the North Carolina coast. Still, the local pilot managed to steer the vessel into the Cape Fear River. Wilmington lay some 25 miles north of the river's mouth.

The night before, another blockade runner, the *Night Hawk*, had gone aground near the mouth of the river. The stricken vessel had then been boarded by Union sailors, and set afire. The blackened hulk that had been the *Night Hawk* now loomed as an obstacle to the *Condor*. In seeking to avoid hitting the sunken vessel, the pilot at the helm of the *Condor* ran the ship aground. The *Condor* sat helplessly, while a small vessel carrying a boarding party of Union sailors approached.

Rose watched tensely as the boat drew closer. She remembered her terrible months of imprisonment in Washington and decided she did not want to repeat that ordeal. She went to the captain and insisted upon having a boat lowered so she could escape. A two-man crew was assigned to row her ashore, and the boat was lowered. Hardly had the boat touched the water when it was caught in a monstrous wave and overturned. The two men managed to cling to the keel of the capsized boat and were rescued, but Rose slipped out of sight. Her body was later washed ashore.

On October 1, 1864, all of Wilmington turned

33

out to watch her funeral procession as it made its way to the grave site. As the coffin was lowered, a full military salute rang out. No one doubted that the South had lost one of its most ardent warriors.

3
Confederate Courier and Agent

Belle Boyd had just turned seventeen and completed her final year at Mount Washington Female College in Baltimore when she was introduced to the reality of the Civil War. The daughter of a storekeeper, Belle, tall and self-assured, was at home in Martinsburg during the summer of 1861 when Northern forces under the command of General Robert Patterson, drifting down through the Shenandoah Valley, began to stream into town. They were there to meet Confederate troops guarding the western approaches to Richmond, the capital of the Confederacy.

For almost a century, Martinsburg had existed as a small, sleepy country village. Then the Baltimore & Ohio Railroad laid its tracks through the valley and built freight yards and repair shops in Martinsburg. (A Virginia community at the time,

Martinsburg remained so until 1863 when West Virginia broke away from Virginia to become a separate state.) As a railroad center, it was a key military objective.

When Patterson's troops entered Martinsburg, the Boyd house was one of the first to be visited by Northern soldiers, who demanded the Union flag be displayed. The demand angered the Boyds, who fiercely supported the Southern cause. "Men," declared Belle's mother, "every member of my household will die before that flag is raised over us." A heated argument followed. One of the soldiers rudely pushed his way past Mrs. Boyd. From the other side of the room, Belle appeared, a thin figure with braided brown hair. She pulled a revolver from her dress and shot him.

Belle was seized and taken to headquarters. The soldier, who is believed to have been Private Frederick Martin, a Pennsylvania volunteer, was taken to the hospital, where he died a few hours later.

Serious charges were brought against Belle, who was taken from her cell to meet the officer in charge of the unit. What was said between 17-year-old Belle and the officer was never recorded, but Belle went unpunished. The officer agreed that she had been provoked, that she had had good reason to do what she had done; she was free to go. Before she left, the officer presented her with a small pistol, a weapon he said she might use in any similar situation.

So began the rebellious career of Belle Boyd, a woman described by historian Douglas Southall

Freeman as "one of the most active and reliable of the many secret women agents of the Confederacy."

It was in Martinsburg that Belle Boyd first began to work for the Confederate cause. Union officers would sometimes leave their pistols and swords in the houses that they occupied. Later they were pained to learn that their weapons had disappeared. No one thought to accuse the youthful and charming Belle Boyd. Still later, the officers were stunned to learn that their pistols and swords had found their way into the hands of Confederate soldiers and were being used against them.

Appropriating Union weapons for Confederate soldiers was only one of Belle's many activities. She spent most of her waking hours gathering information about Union forces. Every scrap of news she could obtain was immediately dispatched to General J. E. B. Stuart and other Confederate officers.

During and after the Battle of Bull Run in the summer of 1861, the first major engagement of the Civil War, Belle played another role. Front Royal, Virginia, west of the battle site, where an aunt of Belle's lived, was established as the site for a Confederate military hospital, and there Belle served as a nurse. Afterward, more than a few wounded soldiers told of the loving care they had received from her.

To the Yankees, Belle showed a very different side of her nature. The Washington *Evening Star* once described her as being "insanely devoted to the rebel cause." She was quick-tempered and feared no one. A youthful aide to General Thomas J. (Stonewall) Jackson once angered her. In a warning she sent to him, Belle declared that if she ever caught him in Martinsburg, she would cut off his ears.

Belle Boyd's most notable feat occurred at Front Royal during the spring of 1862. At the time, General Jackson was conducting a series of raids against federal forces in the Shenandoah Valley of Virginia.

One evening Belle was at her aunt's home in Front Royal, reading to her grandmother and a cousin, when a servant rushed into the room with the news that there were Union soldiers in the streets. Belle sprang to the window and looked out. It was true. The street outside was crowded with Yankee soldiers, milling about in great confusion.

Belle went outside and talked with a federal officer. He explained to her that Confederate forces under generals Jackson and Ewell were approaching the town. "We are endeavoring to get the ordnance and quartermaster's stores out of their reach," he said.

"But what will you do with the stores in the large depot?" Belle asked.

"Burn them, of course!" said the officer.

"But suppose the rebels come upon you too quickly?"

"Then we will fight as long as we can, and in the event of a defeat make good our retreat upon

Winchester, burning the bridges as we cross them . . ."

Belle knew that several Union armies were clustered in the hills and valleys near Front Royal. General Nathaniel Banks' main force was at Strasbourg, General White was at Harpers Ferry, generals James Shields and Geary were a short distance away, and General John C. Fremont was below the valley. Combined, the Union armies outnumbered Jackson two-to-one. By joining together, they could destroy him.

If the retreating Union Army that Jackson was now pursuing was successful in burning the bridges over the Shenandoah River, they would cut off Jackson's means of escape. The combined Union armies would then pounce upon him.

Belle went back inside the house wearing a worried look. From what the officer had told her, she realized a trap was being set for General Jackson and his army. His potential victory at Front Royal could be turned into defeat and disaster.

Belle realized she had to warn Jackson, and there was not a moment to lose. She put on a white sunbonnet and blue dress with a white apron and started running down the main street of Front Royal, which was filled with Union soldiers. Soon she reached the open fields outside of town where the advance units of Jackson's army were firing upon the federal forces as they fell back. "Rifle balls flew thick and fast about me," Belle later wrote, "and more than once struck the ground so near my feet as to throw dirt in my eyes." A shell burst within 20 feet of her, but by throwing herself on the ground she managed to escape injury.

Still under heavy fire, Belle continued to run. As she got close to the Confederate lines, she waved her sunbonnet at the troops. They didn't understand that she was trying to warn them, and simply cheered her.

Then Major Henry Kyd Davis, an aide to General Jackson came riding up to her. "Good God, Belle," he said. "You here! What is it?"

As soon as Belle caught her breath, she told all she knew, how the surrounding hills were filled with Union troops and artillery. For Jackson to be able to escape the trap being set, Belle urged Davis to send a cavalry unit in pursuit of the retreating Federals with orders to seize the bridges before they could destroy them.

The major galloped off to report to General Jackson. Belle returned to Front Royal.

As history has recorded, Jackson's cavalry reached the bridges barely in time to prevent the Federals from blowing them up. Jackson's army then charged into Front Royal, routing the panic-stricken Federals, who fled before they were able to destroy the vast amounts of ammunition and supplies stored there. Jackson captured 9,300 rifles and pistols, 2 cannons, and huge quantities of food and other stores. He had turned the Union plan to trap him into a stunning victory.

After the victory, Jackson did not rest. He pursued the Union Army north to Winchester, where he struck again. Terror now seized the federal forces. Even the city of Washington began to feel threatened.

Soon after the Confederate triumph, Belle received this letter:

> *Miss Belle Boyd:*
> *I thank you for myself and for the army, for the immense service you have rendered your country today.*
> > *Hastily, I am your friend,*
> > *T. J. Jackson, C.S.A.*

Belle prized the letter for the rest of her life.

After her widely publicized activities at Front Royal, Belle continued to act as a courier, carrying messages to Richmond, the Confederate capital. As Union military leaders in Washington began to hear more and more of her exploits, they ordered that she be taken into custody. On July 30, 1862, Belle was arrested and brought under guard to Washington and placed in Old Capitol Prison.

The famous prison, which at one time or another held Rose Greenhow and almost every other person suspected of espionage or conspiracy against the federal government, had been the temporary capitol building of the United States after the British burned Washington in 1814. It was located just east of the present capitol, where the Supreme Court building now stands.

One evening the superintendent of the prison, William B. Wood, visited Belle in her room and asked her to sign an oath of allegiance to the United States government. Belle became enraged. She told Wood, " . . . that if I ever sign one line that will show to the world that I owe to the United States government the slightest allegiance, I hope my arm may fall paralyzed at my side."

"Well," said Wood, "if that is your determination, you'll have to lay here and die."

"Sir, if it is a crime to love the South, its cause, and its President, then I am a criminal," Belle declared. "I am in your power, do with me as you please. But I fear you not. I would rather lie down in this prison and die, than leave it owing allegiance to such a government as yours."

Belle had hardly finished her defiant speech, when cheers and cries of "Bravo!" rang out. The door to her room had been left open during her conversation with Wood, and prisoners in nearby rooms had overheard them.

In the weeks that followed, Belle continued to be an inspiration to her fellow prisoners by singing songs each night that glorified the Confederacy. "Maryland, My Maryland" was one of her favorites. At the sound of her girlish voice, the prison fell silent. One of the other prisoners said, "I have seen men, when she was singing, walk off to one side and pull out their handkerchiefs and wipe their eyes."

Since she had not been charged with any crime, officials eventually had to give Belle her freedom. Late in August 1862, she was released and sent to Richmond, where she was given a hero's welcome.

She became the idol of the Confederacy. On a tour of the Confederate states, she was hailed as the Great Rebel Spy and the Virginia Heroine. When she visited Charleston, South Carolina, General Pierre G.T. Beauregard and his staff held a reception and dinner in her honor.

When her triumphant tour of the South was completed, Belle returned to Martinsburg to visit her mother. Her reputation as a slippery and dangerous agent made Union authorities fearful, and sentries were posted outside of her home with orders to keep her under watch. Before long, she was arrested again and returned to Washington under heavy guard.

This time she was placed in Carroll Prison. When news leaked out that she was there, crowds gathered at night to hear her sing "Take Me Back to My Own Sunny South" and "The Bonny Blue Flag." When she was given permission to exercise in a small park next to the prison, throngs gathered to watch her.

Eventually, Belle was brought before a military court. Its decision was that she be packed off to the South. On December 2, 1863, the New York *Tribune* reported, "Captain James B. Mix of General Martindale's staff left this afternoon for City Point [Virginia] with the notorious Belle Boyd, who is to be delivered to the Rebel authorities at that place." Belle was warned that if she returned to the North, it could mean the firing squad.

The several arrests and two jail terms, and the fact that a death sentence was hanging over her head, about ended Belle's career as a Confederate spy. Realizing this, she offered her services to Jefferson Davis, president of the Confederacy, as a courier. He immediately assigned her to carry important papers to England.

One dark night, Belle, using the alias "Mrs. Lewis," sailed from Wilmington, North Carolina, aboard the *Greyhound*, a blockade-runner flying the British flag. Union ships were waiting for the *Greyhound*. Before dawn broke, the ship had been seized and a Union crew put aboard.

Captain Samuel Hardinge, the handsome young Union naval officer who commanded the boarding party that captured the *Greyhound*, was ordered to sail the ship to New York. On the journey, he was swept off his feet by Belle. Before the *Greyhound* reached New York harbor, he had twice asked Belle to marry him. The first proposal Belle rejected; she accepted the second. Belle had made her captor her captive.

After a brief stop in New York, the *Greyhound* went on to Boston. On May 20, 1864, the Boston *Post* reported the arrival of the *Greyhound*, noting that "the somewhat famous Belle Boyd" was among the passengers. Officers aboard the ship, the paper said, described her as "very ladylike."

It didn't take long for the War Department to realize that Belle Boyd was back. She was taken into custody, but won parole by promising to go to Canada. Soon after, she left Canada for England.

Meanwhile, Captain Hardinge had secured his release from the Navy and he, too, headed for England. He and Belle were married in London at St. James, Piccadilly. Local Confederate sympathizers, many socially prominent Londoners, and scores of the curious attended the ceremony. The date was August 25, 1864. Belle was 21.

Two months after the wedding, Captain Hardinge left his bride and returned to the United States to settle a number of personal matters. He arrived in Brooklyn and then planned to journey south to visit Belle's mother in Martinsburg. But on the way, he was unjustly arrested as a deserter and sent to Washington. He ended up in Carroll Prison, where Belle had once been confined.

Back in London, Belle, with no income, began feeling a financial pinch. She started selling her personal possessions, one by one. Even so, she was forced to move to a dismal boarding house.

But Belle rebounded. She busied herself by writing her autobiogrpahy. It was titled *Belle Boyd in Camp and Prison*, written with help from a London journalist, and was published in both London and New York.

In April 1865, as the Civil War was drawing to an end, Belle returned to the United States to be reunited with her husband. His prison term had left him in a weakened state and he had to be nursed back to health. He never fully recovered. Three years later, he died.

Belle now took to the stage and made a theatrical tour of the South. She appeared in a play, *The Honeymoon*, in New York in 1868. She toured Texas and Ohio.

In 1869, Belle married John V. Hammond, a former British Army officer, and went to live in California. After divorcing Hammond, she married a third husband, Nathaniel High of Toledo, Ohio, in 1885.

Besides her theatrical appearances, Belle was active on the lecture circuit, performing dramatic reenactments of her career as a spy. She billed herself as "The Cleopatra of Secession." Often she was booked at Grand Army Encampments, where she retold her adventures for the assembled veterans and their wives.

Belle died in 1900 in Kilbourn, Wisconsin (now Wisconsin Dells), where she had gone to address members of the Grand Army of the Republic, and was buried there. Each Memorial Day, veterans' groups decorate her grave, not with the Confederate flag, but with the Stars and Stripes.

Belle Boyd must not be resting easily.

4
The Spy Who
Changed Her Color

Women fought side by side with men in the Civil War. They fought not as women but as *men*, disguising themselves by wearing short hair and binding their breasts. Being beardless was not a problem in an army where many soldiers were so young, they had not yet begun to shave.

Some women enlisted to follow husbands, boyfriends, or brothers. Other women joined up because they felt so deeply about the cause they supported. Still others were simply adventurers.

There was great risk in dressing as a man. Any woman found out was looked upon as a misfit and immediately discharged. Mary Scaberry, who took the identity of Charles Freeman during the Civil War, was dismissed from an Ohio regiment when her true sex was discovered after she had been hospitalized for fever. "Sexual incompatability" was given as the official reason for her discharge.

No one knows for certain how many women served as men during the Civil War. Official documents are of little help. For the most part, only those who were discovered have contributed to the record.

Lauren Cook Burgess, a university administrator in North Carolina who collects information about women at war, has evidence that 127 women fought during the Civil War. Most served on the Union side.

The actual figure may have been much higher. Mary L.A. Lawrence of the U.S. Sanitary Commission, a woman's organization during the Civil War that cared for the wounded and sought to raise health standards at camps, in her book *My Story of the War*, written in 1889, said that the number of women soldiers known to be in the service was thought the be "a little less than 400."

Whatever the number, one of the most remarkable of all the female Civil War soldiers was Sarah Emma Edmonds. Using the name Franklin Thompson, Edmonds enlisted in the 2nd Michigan Infantry regiment in 1861 and, as a member of that unit, served with the Army of the Potomac, the main fighting force in the Eastern Theater of operations.

After leaving the army in 1863, Emma wrote of her adventures in a book titled *Nurse and Spy in the Union Army*, which was published in 1865. During her enlistment, Emma — as Franklin Thompson — was either a hospital orderly or a nurse and spent her time helping surgeons and chaplains. In camp and on the battlefield, she distributed mail, carried messages, and helped care for the wounded.

Emma's most exciting adventure was as a spy. For this role, she exchanged her Union uniform for the clothes typically worn by an African-American slave, and blackened her face. The disguise was so convincing that Emma was able to slip through enemy lines, gather information about a Confederate attack and the location of enemy artillery and fortifications, and return to report to Union field commanders.

Some historians have disputed Emmas's incredible tale. But whether she stretched the truth or not, Edmonds is known to have served loyally and fearlessly as a Union soldier, winning praise from her comrades and officers of the regiment.

Sarah Emma Edmonds was Canadian, born in St. John, New Brunswick, in 1839. Her father was an unsmiling and mean-spirited potato farmer, who believed his children had been sent into the world to provide inexpensive farm labor. Hardly out of the cradle, Emma, along with her brothers and sisters, was sent out into the fields to dig and sack potatoes. There were seldom days without toil. When the Edmonds youngsters were permitted to attend school, it was because chores were few.

Despite the harsh life, or perhaps because of it, Emma grew up with an independent spirit and vivid imagination. As a twelve-year-old, she read a book titled *Fanny Campbell, the Female Sailor,* the story of a young British woman who, disguised as a man, enjoyed a life of adventure as a sailor in the Royal Navy. The book made a deep impression on young Emma. She decided that what Fanny had done, she could do.

An opportunity came several years later when Emma was eighteen. Her father announced that he had picked out a husband for her, a man much older than she. For Emma, that was the last straw. With the help of a male friend, she acquired shirts, trousers, and other clothes she needed to dress as a boy, and left home.

Once on her own, Emma marveled at how effective her disguise was. No one seemed to even suspect that she was a girl.

Emma got a job as a traveling Bible salesperson for a Hartford, Connecticut, publisher. In time, she saved enough money to buy a horse and buggy, which enabled her to travel from one village to the next with her store of Bibles.

She once returned to the family farm to visit her mother and sisters. Even they did not recognize her. Her identity was revealed by the family's pet dog who remembered Emma, and whose enthusiastic display of affection aroused everyone's suspicions.

Emma's travels eventually took her to Flint, Michigan, where she boarded with a Methodist minister. By this time, Emma was using the name Franklin Thompson.

During her stay in Flint, Emma became acquainted with William R. Morse, who headed the local militia unit, the Flint Union Greys. When the Civil War broke out in the spring of 1861, Emma is believed to have been encouraged by Morse to join the Greys. Not long after she signed up, the Greys became part of Company F of the 2nd Michigan Volunteer Infantry regiment, which was ordered to depart for Washington, D.C.

The 2nd Michigan Volunteers saw action at Bull Run, also known as Manassas, the first major engagement of the Civil War. Emma served as a male nurse while the battle raged, working with other nurses in caring for the wounded.

Early in 1862, General George McClellan shifted the mighty Army of the Potomac to Fort Monroe, Virginia, to launch the Peninsular Campaign, which had the Confederate capital of Richmond as its goal. McClellan's huge army included the 2nd Michigan Volunteers. Emma, still as Franklin Thompson, was assigned to collect and distribute the regimental mail. She was later promoted to brigade postmaster.

Emma's assignment gave her freedom of movement about the camp, the chance to wander about and visit hospitals, where she helped to attend the sick and wounded. That was the type of duty she preferred.

One morning, a scouting party returned to camp with a Confederate prisoner who revealed that a Union spy had been captured in Richmond and was about to be hanged. Union military leaders wanted a replacement. Emma decided to apply for the assignment, even though a chaplain described it as "a situation of great danger and responsibility."

Emma's name was sent to headquarters, and soon after she was asked to appear for an interview. An officer asked her about her knowledge of firearms, her political views, and the reasons for wanting to take such a dangerous job. Upon answering the questions satisfactorily, Emma was given an oath of allegiance and commissioned as a spy in the Union Army.

She was given three days to prepare for her first assignment, which involved adopting a disguise and making her way through enemy lines to the city of Richmond, the rebel capital. There was no CIA in those days, no federal espionage organization to provide a fake identity for a person about to embark on an undercover assignment. It was left to Emma to create her own disguise.

Emma was already masquerading as a man. Now she decided she would change her race as well and assume the identity of a black slave.

Emma realized that posing as a slave was the perfect way to conceal herself. Slaves were everywhere in the South. Slightly more than one third of the Confederacy's 9,000,000 people were black slaves. Most Southerners looked upon them as "faithful retainers," as individuals to be used. As such, there was little concern for them. To the white Southerner, in fact, black slaves were practically invisible.

It was easier for Emma to change her sex than

her race. She first bought a "suit of contraband [slave] clothing, real plantation style," and then went to a barber who cropped her hair close to her head. That was merely the beginning.

The next step was to change her skin color. She obtained a vial of silver nitrate, a powder that turned her head, neck, face, and hands "black as any African."

To complete her transformation, Emma needed a wig, but there was none to be had at Fort Monroe. The nearest wig supplier was in Washington. So when a Washington-bound mailboat docked at Fort Monroe, Edmonds asked the postmaster aboard to purchase a wig for her. Once he returned from the capital, wig in hand, Emma was ready to begin her adventure.

When Emma set out on foot for Richmond, she carried no pack of supplies, not even a blanket, nothing that would arouse suspicion. She had a few hard crackers in her pocket and a loaded pistol in her belt. By 9:30 that first night, she had passed through the outer lines of the Union defenses and by midnight she was behind rebel lines. Not once was she stopped by a sentry. At one point, she had passed to within ten feet of a Confederate guard, and he had not noticed her.

Once she was well behind rebel lines, Edmonds stretched out on the cold, damp ground and rested. The first thing that caught her eye in the morning was a party of slaves carrying hot coffee and food to rebel troops. Emma quickly became friendly with the group and was given a mug of coffee and a piece of cornbread. When the slaves returned from their mission, she joined them. They were on their way back to Yorktown, she was told. She was relieved to realize that not a single member of the group seemed the least bit suspicious of her.

When they reached Yorktown, the slaves reported to an overseer who ordered them back to work building fortifications. Edmonds didn't know what to do. Her bewilderment changed to anxiety when an officer came up to her and asked, "Who do you belong to, and why are you not at work?"

Using a dialect she had been practicing, Emma explained she was free, that she didn't belong to anyone and was heading for Richmond to seek work.

The officer scowled. "Take that black rascal and set him to work," he shouted to one of the overseers, "and if he won't work well, tie him up and give him twenty lashes."

Emma was made to join a force of more than a hundred slaves at work building defensive fortifications. They were part of a huge army of slaves used by the Confederate and state governments to prepare the Confederacy for Union attacks. Other blacks drove supply wagons or served as ambulance drivers. Blacks also were stretcher bearers and hospital attendants. Thousands worked on railroads in the South, keeping the lines repaired. Those in the party Emma was forced to join built gun emplacements and dug earthworks.

Emma was supplied with a shovel, pickax, and what she called a "monstrous wheelbarrow." Her job was to help in the construction of an earthen and gravel embankment, about eight feet in height, which was to shield Confederate troops from Union fire. Once the wheelbarrow was loaded with gravel, Emma had to push it up a plank to the top of the wall and empty it. Often, as the wheelbarrow was about to lurch off the plank, another slave would rush to help her. At the end of the day, Emma's hands were sore and blistered "from my wrists to the finger ends."

When darkness fell, Emma and the other slaves were free to go where they pleased within the camp. Emma used her freedom to tour the rebel positions and make an inventory of the fortifications, particularly the mounted guns. She jotted down this information in a brief report together with a sketch of the fort's outer boundaries and tucked it into the sole of her shoe. Then she returned to the slaves' quarters.

Emma's second day as a Confederate slave was much easier than the first. Since her hands were not strong enough to handle a wheelbarrow or shovel much earth, she changed jobs with a young slave who carried water to the troops. She offered the young man five dollars in federal greenbacks to make the switch, but he said he could not take the money.

The job gave her the opportunity to listen to the soldiers discussing military matters. She learned how many reinforcements the rebels were expecting and she got to see General Robert E. Lee, who was there to inspect the Union fortifications and hold a council of war with General Joseph E. Johnston. At the time, Lee commanded the Army of Virginia. He later was given overall command of all the Confederate armies.

Later in the day, Emma brought some water to her friends in the slave quarters. As they were enjoying a cool drink, one of the slaves looked at her in a puzzled manner, then turned to one of his friends and said, "Jim, I'll be darned if that feller ain't turnin' white!"

Emma's heart skipped a beat. But she managed to grin and say, "Well, I always been expectin' to come white some time; my mother's white."

The simple remark drew laughter from her companions, and the subject was dropped.

As soon as she got a chance, Emma took a look at herself in a small pocket mirror she carried. The slave had been right, she was beginning to turn white. Emma quickly applied more silver nitrate powder from a vial she carried.

When Emma returned to the company to which she had been assigned with more water, she saw a group of soldiers gathered about a man who was talking excitedly. Emma went up to the group quietly, put down the cans of water she had been carrying, and started filling the soldiers' canteens. She thought the voice of the man who was doing all the talking sounded familiar. When she glanced at him, she immediately recognized him as a peddler who used to come to the federal camp at least

Lydia Darragh delivers her secret message to Colonel Craig.

Rose Greenhow and her daughter, "Little Rose," pose outside Old Capitol Prison for Mathew Brady.

Belle Boyd in the late 1870's.

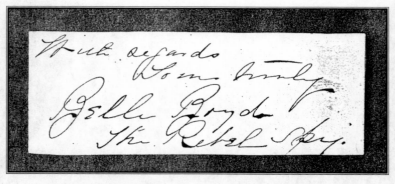

In granting a request for an autograph, Belle Boyd identified herself as "The Rebel Spy."

Under the name of Franklin Thompson,
Sarah Emma Edmonds served with the
Union Army for two years.

Emma Edmonds as
Franklin Thompson.

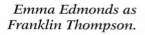

Mata Hari, the world-famous dancer and spy.

During World War I, this poster warned Navy personnel to be on guard against female spies.

A copy of Ruth Kuehn Moore's "Basic Personnel Report" from the files of the Crystal City, Texas, Internment Camp, where she was held in custody.

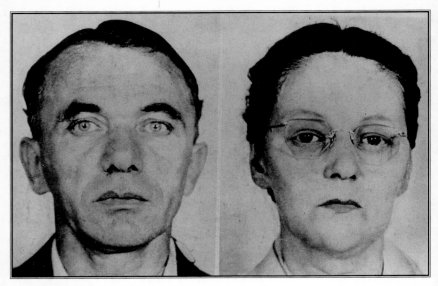

Bernard Kuehn and his wife Friedel as pictured in 1943.

Japanese attack on Pearl Harbor brought death to some 2,400 Americans.

Lily Belard, The Cat, has a word with her lawyer during her trial in Paris.

The secret headquarters of Interallié in Paris.

SECRET

TABLEAUX B

CHIFFRANT

A UTILISER AVIC C G N
(CAHIER B)

EXEMPLAIRE N° 125

Cover of the code book stolen
and copied by Betty Pack.

A bridal portrait of Betty Pack.

once a week selling newspapers and stationery. He would hang around, Emma recalled, for half a day at a time.

Emma was astounded by what the man was saying. He gave the troops a complete description of the federal fortifications and McClellan's army. He even had a map that he exhibited. The peddler-spy boasted of how he had overheard that one of the officers from headquarters planned to visit the outer line of Union troops. He relayed the information to rebel sharpshooters. They waited for the officer. When he appeared, they shot him dead.

Emma later wrote:

> *I thanked God for that information. I would willingly have wrought with those Negroes on that parapet for two months, and have worn the skin off my hands half a dozen times, to have gained that single item. He was a fated man from that moment; his life was not worth three cents in Confederate scrip. But fortunately he did not know the feelings that agitated the heart of that little black urchin who sat there so quietly filling those canteens, and it was well that he did not.*

On the evening of her third day in camp, Emma was sent with other slaves to carry supper to the outer line of rebel troops. Known as the picket line, it was made up of troops posted at regular intervals whose job it was to warn against a Union advance. Some of the men on duty on the picket line were slaves.

While Emma and the other slaves were handing out food to the pickets, the Union troops, who were less than half a mile away, opened fire. "Yankee Minie balls were whistling around our heads," Emma later recalled.

During the encounter, a Confederate officer patroling the picket line on horseback approached Emma and wanted to know what she was doing there. Emma explained that she was one of the slaves that had brought supper to the troops and that she was waiting for the Union troops to stop firing before she started back.

"You come along with me," said the officer.

Emma trailed behind the officer for almost a quarter of a mile, until they came to a Confederate petty officer. "Put this man in the post where that man was shot until I return," the officer ordered.

Emma was given a rifle and told to use it freely should anything or anyone approach from the other side. Before leaving, the petty officer said, "Now, you black rascal, if you sleep on your post, I'll shoot you like a dog!"

Emma was much too frightened to even think of sleeping.

It was a dark, overcast night. It started to rain. Emma noted that the pickets on either side of her had taken shelter under the trees. When she saw they weren't looking, Emma darted forward toward the Union lines, carrying the rifle as a prize.

She knew the Union pickets would fire at anyone approaching, so she spent the remainder of the night in a wooded area, as close to the Union lines as she dared to get. At daybreak, she signaled to the Union soldiers and was welcomed by them.

Emma immediately made out her report and took it to General McClellan's headquarters, where she was heartily congratulated. The rifle that she brought back with her was sent to Washington where it was displayed in the Capitol as a trophy of the war.

According to her book, *Nurse and Spy*, that was Emma's only attempt at spying during the Civil War. At the battle of Antietam (Maryland), which took place on September 17, 1862, and is known as "the bloodiest single day of the Civil War," Emma was a nurse once again.

Four women are known to have fought at Antietam. Emma later wrote of coming upon a severely wounded soldier at Antietam who was a female in disguise. "Something in the tone and voice made me look closely at the face," Emma wrote. She said the dying soldier revealed her identity and asked Edmonds to bury her and keep her secret.

During the battle of Fredricksburg (Virginia), in December 1862, Emma was assigned as an orderly to General Orlando Poe, carrying messages and orders for him. Poe later had high praise for his orderly, saying she "carried messages through showers of shot and shell with a fearlessness that attracted the attention and secured the commendation of field and general officers."

Emma left the service in 1863, receiving a medical discharge after she became ill with malaria. Once she regained her health, she served as a female nurse in hospitals around Harpers Ferry, Virginia.

Once the war was over, Emma returned to her family's home in New Brunswick. There she renewed her friendship with Linus Seelye, who, as a boy, had given her the clothes she had used to first disguise herself. She and Linus fell in love and were married. The couple had three children, all of whom died in infancy.

In 1882, or thereabouts, Emma applied to the federal government for retirement benefits due her for the time she served with the United States Army. She was asked to supply written statements from the officers and men of the 2nd Michigan Volunteers who knew of her service and would be willing to support her claim. Through her letters to them, several of Emma's old comrades became aware for the first time of the true identity of Franklin Thompson.

In 1884, to further her pension claim, Emma attended a reunion of the regiment in Flint, Michigan. A local newspaper reported, "The slender and wiry Frank Thompson of 1863 now appeared as a woman of about medium height, and had grown rather stout and fleshy."

A special Congressional committee was appointed to examine her claim, which was eventually approved. Emma was granted a pension of twelve dollars a month "for her sacrifices in the line of duty, her splendid record as a soldier, her unblemished character and disabilities incurred in the service."

5
The Legendary Mata Hari

More than three quarters of a century have passed since a French firing squad put an end to the life of Mata Hari for her activities as a German spy. With her death, she became a legend. To this day, when the subject is women spies, Mata Hari is likely to be the first name mentioned.

The story of Mata Hari as the most beautiful and mysterious spy of all time has been romanticized and popularized in countless articles and books and by a Hollywood feature film starring the fabled Greta Garbo. No other spy has been so glamorized.

Yet the truth is that Mata Hari was not a great spy. Her legend was created by her own lies and by a French government anxious to build a case against her. Tabloid newspapers and Hollywood scriptwriters took it from there.

Concerning her early life, however, the facts are clear. Her real name was Margareta Gertrude Zelle, and her parents were Dutch. She was born in the town of Leeuwarden in northern Holland on August 7, 1876, and was known as Gerda as a child. Her mother was from a prominent Dutch family, while her father, who was good-looking but bad-tempered, was a moderately successful hatter.

When Gerda was 14, her mother died and she and her father moved to Amsterdam. Tall, dark, and somewhat exotic-looking, Gerda was often taken to be three or four years older than her actual age. Men were drawn to her and she, in turn, was fascinated by them.

Gerda decided she wanted to become a schoolteacher. At 17, she entered a teachers' training college. She had been in school only a short time when the dean fell in love with her. Gerda immediately left school and went to live with an aunt in The Hague.

Gerda met the man who was to become her first husband when she was 18. He was 39-year-old Rudolph MacLeod, a captain in the Dutch Army. While on leave from his post in the Dutch East Indies, MacLeod's friends kidded him for never having married. One of them placed an advertisement for a wife for him in a Dutch newspaper. One of the replies the ad attracted was from Gerda. Within six days after their first meeting, they were engaged. They got married before the end of the year.

The 18-year-old woman and the army officer

more than twice her age were completely unsuited for each other. He was quiet and cultured, a gentleman. Gerda, like her father, was selfish and bad-tempered. Luxury was what she liked. She quickly spent all of MacLeod's money.

Within a year or so of the wedding, their marriage was on the verge of breaking up. Then MacLeod was offered a promotion and an important assignment in Java in the Dutch East Indies. Gerda and their son went to Java with him. A daughter was born while the couple was there.

Gerda had little interest in the people, ancient culture, or magnificent scenery of Java. Men were her passion. She became romantically involved with other men, including officers on her husband's staff. In later years, she accused her husband of drunkenness and treating her brutally and threatening her life with a revolver. Adding to their woes, their son died.

Late in 1902, after the MacLeods returned to Holland, the couple split up. Rudolph was given custody of their daughter.

With her newly won freedom, Gerda, at the age of 27, decided to go to Paris to seek her fortune. She tried modeling but did not have much success.

While in the East Indies, Gerda had become fascinated by the religious dances of the beautiful Javanese women. In private, she began to develop her own version of these dances. When she demonstrated her artistry at a party, she was spotted by a well-known figure in the Paris theatrical world. He provided her with professional advice and introduced her to people willing to help her. Soon after, Gerda MacLeod vanished to be replaced by an overnight sensation in the world of late-night entertainment in Paris. Her name was Mata Hari.

A Mata Hari performance could raise an audience to near frenzy. A strange perfume hung in the air. Music, as though from a snake-charmer's pipe, fell upon the ear. The curtain rose to reveal a dimly lit giant Buddha surrounded by a mass of silken gold-and-silver draperies. From behind the shimmering silk, Mata Hari began to dance. Her eyes were half-closed, her long, thin body, adorned by glittering chains and necklaces of gleaming stones, moved, as one observer put it, "as Paris had never seen one move before."

To go with her exotic career, Mata Hari created a remarkable story about her life. She told friends and admirers that she had been born in southern India, "on the Malabar coast." Her father had been a holy man; her mother, a temple dancer who had died on the day her daughter was born. The daughter had been raised by a temple priest and given the name Mata Hari — Eye of the Morning.

For years, Mata Hari had danced in the great pagoda of Siva and on the granite altar of the temple of Kanda-Swany. One day she had been seen by a handsome young British officer, who was overwhelmed by her beauty. He had stolen her from the temple priests and married her. A son born to the couple had been poisoned by a native servant, whom Mata Hari had strangled with her own hands. Then her husband had died of malaria. She could never return to her homeland, so she had come to Paris to reveal the secrets of the exotic religious dances of the East.

Mata Hari danced in Vienna and was invited to Berlin. She created an even greater stir in the German capital than in Paris.

She was entertained by many highly placed Germans. There were rumors that she became romantically involved with Crown Prince Wilhelm, known to the British as "Little Willie." Wilhelm was said to be so madly in love with Mata Hari that he took her with him to the German Army maneuvers held each fall in Silesia.

By 1913, when Mata Hari was 37, she was still an attractive woman, but her career as a dancer had virtually ended. From this point on, hard facts about her life are difficult to establish.

War clouds were gathering in Europe. The Germans and French were soon to take up arms against one another in what would become World War I. Sometime during this period, Mata Hari was recruited as a German spy. She may have made the move because she was no longer popular as a dancer or it may have been she was seeking a new and exciting life.

In the final weeks of July 1914, Mata Hari was in Berlin. Three nights before the first shots were fired in World War I, she was seen dining in a Berlin restaurant with Herr van Jagow, head of the Prussian secret police. This organization would one day become the Gestapo, the infamous

German internal security agency. Mata Hari received the handsome sum of 30,000 marks (about $12,000 dollars) from van Jagow, who registered her as agent H.21.

From Berlin, Mata Hari went to Belgium, Holland, England, and Paris, and from there, after a time, to the battlefront. She stayed in the town of Vittel, which was within the military zone, for several months disguised as a nurse. It was not a difficult matter for a beautiful nurse to gain the confidence of French officers, and from them she obtained valuable military information for the Germans.

An uninterrupted flow of dispatches went from Mata Hari to the Dutch Embassy in Paris, where it was believed she was corresponding with her relatives in Holland. Instead, the messages ended up in the hands of German intelligence in Amsterdam. The dispatches were then sent on to Berlin.

It has been said that Mata Hari obtained details of the famous French defense plan XVII from her French military contacts, and relayed this information to the Germans. She is also credited with warning German military leaders of the French offensive on the Chemin des Dames and the British plan to attack the Somme.

The British secret service was the first to become aware of Mata Hari's activities, and alerted the French. When Mata Hari realized she was under suspicion and being watched, she left the war zone and returned to Paris. But even there, she did not feel safe. Therefore, she did what other spies have done when involved in similar circumstances: She offered her services to the other side.

To show her good faith, she gave the French details of points off the coast of Morocco where German submarines were concealed — information the French already happened to have.

The French knew it would be invaluable to have a spy operating within the German high command. But they were not convinced that Mata Hari could be trusted. To find out, they set a trap for her. Pretending to accept her offer, they proposed that her first mission involve a trip to German-occupied Belgium. She was given a list of six names and told they were agents she could use in sending information back to Paris. Five of the names were fake names. The sixth was a French spy. If Mata Hari was still loyal to the Germans, she would pass on the six names to German intelligence.

Three weeks later, the French spy was shot by the Germans. Only Mata Hari could have betrayed him.

The French did not arrest her, and she was allowed to leave France. Some time later, Mata Hari appeared in Madrid. There she contacted the German secret service and offered to work for the Germans once again. But the Germans had doubts about her, too. And even if she did happen to be loyal to the Germans, she was now too well known, too closely watched.

German secret service officers in Madrid sent a

telegram to intelligence headquarters asking for guidance. The reply instructed Mata Hari — agent H.21 — to return to France and continue her mission. A Paris bank was instructed to issue her a check in the amount of 5,000 francs.

Mata Hari went to France to pick up the money. It's been said that in communicating with her, the Germans used an old code, one that the French had broken. If this is true, Mati Hari was practically handed over to the French by the Germans.

Almost the minute she arrived in Paris, Mata Hari was seized by the French police. When she was taken into custody and searched, she was found to be carrying documents that confirmed she was a secret agent for the Germans. She also had in her possession a vial of oxycyanide of mercury, a chemical often used as "invisible ink."

Mata Hari could not have picked a worse time to be arrested. The war was going badly for the French and their generals were looking for a scapegoat to explain their military disasters. Mata Hari fit that role nicely.

Within a week after her arrest, her trial began. It was said that she had managed to obtain all the secrets of the French military from officers swept away by her beauty and charm. The information she passed on to the Germans, said the prosecutor, resulted in the death of some 50,000 French soldiers and sailors. No proof was offered to support the accusation.

Mata Hari did admit that she worked for the Germans, but claimed to be a spy in name only.

Her true loyalties, she said, lay with the French.

But the French believed otherwise, and found her guilty. During World War I, it was usual for the French to execute enemy spies, and Mata Hari's case was to be no exception. She was sentenced to death by a firing squad, a verdict she accepted calmly.

Close to three months passed before the sentence was carried out; Mata Hari fully expected that she would be pardoned. But the French turned a deaf ear to her appeals and those of her lawyer.

The sentence was to be carried out on October 15, 1917. A little after 5 A.M., she was awakened by prison guards and told that the president of France had rejected her final appeal. Her hour of execution was at hand. "It is not possible," she was heard to say, over and over.

Sister Léonide, a French nun who was to accompany her to the execution site, began to quietly weep. "Do not fear, sister," Mata Hari said. "I will know how to die without weakening. You will see a beautiful death."

Mata Hari was led to an automobile that was to take her to Vincennes, where the firing squad waited. The car reached Vincennes as dawn was breaking. As Mata Hari was taken from the car, Sister Léonide and a priest followed, praying.

Two soldiers positioned her against a tall post and fastened her hands behind it. She refused to allow them to cover her eyes with a handkerchief. The firing squad shouldered their rifles and marched to within ten paces of where she stood. Mata Hari smiled. The officer in charge of the firing party raised his sword and the soldiers took aim. Drums rolled. Then, slow and sharp, came the command "Fire!" As the report died away, she slumped forward and fell to the ground — and the legend of Mata Hari was born.

6
Family of Spies

It was one of the bigget shocks in the history of warfare. Early on the morning of December 7, 1941, a sunny Sunday, hundreds of carrier-based Japanese torpedo-carrying planes and dive bombers launched a sudden and unexpected attack on the Pearl Harbor naval base and other U.S. military installations on the Hawaiian island of Oahu.

As the Japanese planes approached their targets, Commander Mitsuo Fuchida, who led the attack, scanned the blue morning sky and noted that no American planes had taken to the air to defend Oahu. And where was the antiaircraft fire? The Japanese had achieved maximum strategic surprise. Fuchida bent forward to speak into his radio transmitter. *"Tora! Tora! Tora!"* ("Tiger! Tiger! Tiger!") his voice rang out. These were the code words to the entire Japanese Navy that meant the

American Pacific Fleet had been caught napping.

Battleships were at anchor, lined up like sitting ducks. Bombers and fighters were parked on airstrips in neat rows.

The United States paid heavily for its lack of alertness. In the two hours the attack lasted, more than 2,400 Americans were killed, over a thousand were wounded, and 18 ships and 188 aircraft were destroyed.

The attack was so unexpected that American defenders were able to shoot down only 29 enemy aircraft. Fewer than one hundred of the Japanese attackers were killed.

The sneak attack on Pearl Harbor jolted Americans as had nothing before or since. The day after the attack, President Franklin D. Roosevelt went before a joint session of Congress and called for a declaration of war against Japan. December 7, 1941, he said, was "a date which will live in infamy."

Around noon on the very same Monday that President Roosevelt was addressing the joint session of Congress, two members of U.S. Military Intelligence in Hawaii were driving to the village of Kalama on Lanakai Bay on the Hawaiian island of Oahu. On the road to Kalama, the two men could see oily black smoke rising from the smoldering wreckage in the harbor.

In Kalama, the agents stopped before the home of Dr. Bernard Julius Otto Kuehn. Dr. Kuehn himself, his wife Friedel, and his stepdaughter, Ruth, had been suspected of espionage for some time.

Taken to headquarters, the Kuehns were questioned. At first, they denied any involvement with the Japanese government. But Dr. Kuehn eventually signed a statement saying that he and his family were Japanese espionage agents. The Kuehns had prepared the way for the Japanese bombers.

After a thorough investigation, American intelligence officials reconstructed the story of the Kuehn family and their involvement in the attack on Pearl Harbor. Bernard Kuehn was born in Germany forty-seven years before. When he was eighteen, he had enlisted in the German Navy and had served aboard a German cruiser during World War I. When the vessel was sunk by a British battleship, Kuehn was rescued and sent to a prisoner-of-war camp in England. There he spent the remainder of the war and mastered the English language.

After the war, Kuehn became a doctor and also an early member of the Nazi Party, which, under Adolf Hitler, seized political control of Germany in 1933. Dr. Kuehn also belonged to the German Navy's secret police.

In 1935, Dr. Kuehn met with Captain Tado Yokoi, a high-ranking Japanese naval official, in Berlin. As a result of the meeting, Dr. Kuehn agreed to become a spy for the Japanese. He signed a contract that stated he would receive a salary of $2,000 a month and a bonus of $6,000 at the end of each year.

Soon after, Dr. Kuehn and his family were sent to Japan to learn Japanese. While there, Dr. Kuehn was interviewed by Captain Kanji Ogawa, Chief of American Affairs of Japanese Intelligence. Ogawa approved the hiring of Dr. Kuehn, but not without some misgivings. To Captain Ogawa, Dr. Kuehn seemed a bit too timid and high-strung for the important assignment he was to be given.

Despite their doubts, the Japanese sent Dr. Kuehn and his wife, and their son, Eberhard, and stepdaughter, Ruth, to Hawaii late in 1935. The Kuehns bought property there and settled down for a long stay. Dr. Kuehn claimed to be a professor of anthropology. He had come to Hawaii, he said, to study the influence of the Japanese people upon the territory's Polynesian culture. Looked upon as well-to-do people of charm and refinement, the Kuehns were warmly welcomed by their Hawaiian neighbors.

Ruth became very popular. An attractive young woman with a soft German accent, she captivated countless American naval officers stationed at Pearl Harbor, the hub of U.S. naval power in the Pacific. She also made friends with officers from many of the naval vessels that used Pearl Harbor as a home port.

War had been raging in Asia, beginning with Japan's attack on China in 1937. While most Americans sympathized with the Chinese, it did not seem likely that the United States would enter the war.

Besides China, Japan's goals for expansion included Thailand, Malayasia, the Netherlands Indies, and the Philippines. But the U.S. Navy's

Pacific Fleet loomed as a serious stumbling block to the Japanese should they seek to achieve their goals. To Admiral Isoroku Yamamoto, the American Pacific Fleet was "a dagger pointed at the throat of Japan."

While the Japanese planned their next move, the forces of Adolf Hitler were on the march. On September 1, 1939, Germany attacked Poland. After crushing the Poles, the German war machine overran six other countries by June 1940 — Denmark, Norway, Belgium, Luxembourg, the Netherlands, and France.

The Japanese looked on in admiration and awe. Before the end of the year, the Japanese had entered into an agreement with Germany and Italy to create the Axis powers. "Japan," said Yosuke Matsuoka, the nation's foreign minister, "should push boldly forward, hand in hand with Germany," not hestitating to commit "double suicide" with the Germans if it became necessary.

By September 1941, Japan's military leaders had made a decision to prepare to fight the United States. Plans were drawn up for a carrier strike force to hit Pearl Harbor before the end of the year.

For the attack to be successful, the Japanese needed information about American warships. Specifically, it was essential for the Japanese to be informed at least two weeks in advance whether the United States Fleet would be in Pearl Harbor on the day designated for the attack.

Japanese Naval Intelligence was given the responsibility of providing the information. And Japanese Naval Intelligence then turned to the Kuehns.

Ruth Kuehn had opened a beauty parlor that catered to the wives of the officers on the ships that made up the Pacific Fleet. These women, whose lives were closely connected to the comings and goings of their husbands or boyfriends, unintentionally provided vital bits and pieces of information about the movements of individual ships. Ruth's mother, Friedel, helped out at the beauty shop, providing another pair of ears for eavesdropping.

Dr. Kuehn had bought two houses that served the family as listening posts. One was a beach house at Kalama at Lanakai Bay near the southeastern corner of Oahu. The house had a steeply sloping roof with a dormer window, which could be seen by vessels many miles out at sea. From the window, Ruth made regular reports to submarines using a coded signal system of flashing lights devised by her father. The submarines then relayed the messages to Japan. Another method of communicating with the Japanese involved the careful arrangement of pieces of white linen on the beach in front of the Kuehn house.

What the Kuehns had been doing had not gone unnoticed. Their activities had come to the attention of the District Intelligence Office (DIO) in Hawaii. By early 1939, the Kuehns had been singled out by the DIO as probable agents for either the Japanese or Germans, or perhaps both. But authorities made no plans to arrest them. After all, the United States was at peace.

On November 22, 1941, the Japanese task force of 31 warships, which included 6 aircraft carriers, 2 battleships, plus cruisers, destroyers, and submarines assembled near the Kurile Islands, far to the north of Hawaii. Four days later, as the massive fleet headed south, orders were received to strike on December 7.

In the week before the attack, a Japanese naval intelligence officer in Hawaii met with Dr. Kuehn and Ruth. They worked out a system of light signals the Kuehns would use to flash information to a Japanese submarine concerning the United States Fleet at Pearl Harbor. The submarine would then relay the message to Tokyo. From there, the message would be transmitted to the commanding officer of the task force.

Using the coded flashing lights, the Kuehns disclosed to the Japanese that there were eight battleships in port, not including the *Pennsylvania*, which was in drydock. A heavy cruiser, six light cruisers, and numerous destroyers and auxiliary ships were also there. The Japanese were disappointed to learn that the Navy's aircraft carriers based at Pearl Harbor had put out to sea. The Kuehns also informed the Japanese that no protective screen of blimps surrounded the ships.

Just before dawn on December 7, the Japanese fleet reached a point about 200 miles north of the Hawaiian Islands. At 6 A.M., the huge bomber force began taking off from the Japanese carriers.

Shortly before 8 o'clock, the bombers made their first run over the island of Oahu. Pilots could see the eight battleships and other vessels, as reported by the Kuehns. Within minutes, three battleships had been blown up or sunk, another had toppled over, and a fifth was heavily damaged. Many other warships were sunk or crippled. Before the Japanese planes returned to their carriers, they managed to wreck the bulk of the U.S. Pacific Fleet.

What happened at Pearl Harbor also served to rouse the American people. Millions of American men and women were mobilized in the armed forces. On the home front, millions of others produced the airplanes, tanks, guns, and other weapons that brought about the eventual defeat of Japan, Germany, and Italy. So while the Pearl Harbor attack was a great tragedy for America, in the end it helped to trigger the defeat of the Axis powers.

On the night following the Pearl Harbor attack, the Kuehns were to be picked up by a Japanese submarine and whisked to safety. But they were arrested before they had a chance to flee.

Tried in 1942 before a military court and found guilty of espionage against the United States, Dr. Kuehn was sentenced to be executed by a firing squad. His sentence was later reduced to fifty years in prison, of which he served only four. After his release from prison, Dr. Kuehn was held on Ellis Island in New York harbor. In December 1948, he left for Argentina, where he planned to live.

Ruth Kuehn and her stepmother did not receive

prison sentences, but were merely held in custody, that is, interned, until the war ended in 1945. During the time she was interned, Ruth sought and received a divorce from J. Carson Moore, a retired stockbroker from New York, whom she had married early in 1941.

Ruth and her mother were deported to Germany after World War II. Considering the dimensions of the Pearl Harbor disaster and its tragic nature, and the part that Kuehns played in it, it is curious that they got off so lightly. Countless spies have paid with their lives for accomplishing far less.

7
The Cat

On a bone-chilling rainy day in January 1949, curious Parisians crowded into a drab courtroom for the sentencing of Lily Carré. Small and quiet, with a fringe of hair combed forward over her forehead, Carré, who was French, spied for both the French and Germans during World War II, and is believed to have betrayed them both. French patriots who were her comrades ended up in Nazi concentration camps because of her treachery. "That girl lies with the same ease as she breathes," it was said.

One British agent said, "For Lily, resistance and espionage work, which we found to be a difficult and hazardous business, were like child's play."

She was born Mathilde-Lucie Belard on June 29, 1908, in Creusot in central France. To the family, she was known as Lily.

Her father, an engineer, always dreamed of leaving Creusot, a small and grimy factory town. Not long after Lily's birth, he did so. He and Lily's mother settled in Paris. Lily was sent to live with her 79-year-old grandfather and two unmarried aunts.

With dark-hair, thin lips, and big green eyes, Lily was bright and lively as a young girl. Her schooling included four years at a boarding school, which she described as "a kind of prison." She hated it. At the age of sixteen, with boarding school behind her, Lily rejoined her parents in Paris.

She continued her education at the Sorbonne, a university in Paris. She wanted to become a doctor, but her mother told her the study of medicine was not proper for a young girl. Lily switched to law. She also studied the piano, singing, and developed a fondness for French literature. Later, she decided against law and became a teacher instead.

During her college years, Lily was popular with male students and had many boyfriends, some much older than she. Two of them proposed marriage to her. One was Marc, a law school teacher. He was tall and intelligent, with perfect manners. The other was Maurice, also a teacher, handsome and athletic, with a taste for the modern theater and classical music.

Unable to make up her mind, Lily flipped a coin to decide. If it came down heads, she would marry Marc; tails and it would be Maurice. The coin came down tails.

Lily married Maurice Carré secretly, without telling her parents. Not long after, Maurice was appointed principal of a school at Algeria in North Africa. Lily was to be one of the teachers. It was an unusual experience and she delighted in it.

As the years passed, however, Lily grew unhappy. Life was monotonous and dull, too organized for her.

But great change was coming. Adolf Hitler had risen to power in Germany. The French government began to give in to the demands of the Nazi leader.

Germany invaded Poland on September 1, 1939, triggering World War II. Two days later, France and Great Britain declared war on Germany. Maurice was called into the service and sent to Syria.

Alone in Algeria, Lily managed to reach France aboard a troopship and went to live with her parents in Versailles, not far from Paris, where her father, a lieutenant in the French reserve, was stationed.

Lily decided to become a nurse and started training. In the spring of 1940, she was serving at a hospital in Beauvais in the north of France. It was at this time that the Germans, having conquered Poland, launched a massive offensive, attacking Belgium, Luxembourg, and the Netherlands, then invading France through Belgium. French resistance quickly melted before the German onslaught. Lily was caught up in the great retreat of the French Army.

Lily was in the south of France in mid-June when she heard the news that German soldiers had marched into Paris. Shortly after, the French signed an armistice with the Germans. Under its terms, the Germans were to occupy the northern two thirds of France, while the south would remain under French control.

The war left Lily with many bitter memories. She remembered working night and day in Beauvais and dying men being brought to the hospital in every kind of vehicle — even wheelbarrows. She remembered being attacked by German bombers and fleeing machine-gun fire by German infantrymen on her flight south.

Lily was determined to continue fighting for France. A vast resistance movement of French patriots was being organized, and Lily wanted to become part of it.

In September 1940, Lily and a girlfriend were dining at a restaurant in Toulouse. At the next table sat a dark, handsome man with a scarred face who kept smiling at her. When Lily left the restaurant, he followed her and asked if he might see her home. Lily said no. But when the man insisted on seeing her the next day, she agreed.

At the Café Tortoni, the man told her he was a Polish Air Force officer named Roman Czeriavsky. He said he had fought the Germans, been taken prisoner, and had managed to escape to southern France. He complained that he had difficulty speaking and writing French. Lily said she would help him improve.

As Lily and Roman became better acquainted, he revealed to her that he was part of a Polish intelligence network that was in contact with the British Secret Service in London. He had been chosen to go to Paris and set up a new network with headquarters there. But because he spoke French so poorly, he needed someone he could trust who would be able to keep contact with the network's French-speaking agents. Would Lily want to take on this job? It sounded exciting, exactly like something she wanted to do. She began to imagine herself as a modern Mata Hari, an alluring woman whose exploits as a clever spy would earn her a place in history.

When the French Secret Service learned of Roman and Lily and their plans to establish a Polish spy network in Paris, they asked Lily to become a double agent and report to them as well. Lily readily agreed. She was given an agent's number and brief training in espionage work in Vichy. This included the use of codes and instruction in identifying different units of the German Army by the colors and insignia they wore.

Lily also learned how to manufacture and use "invisible ink." The "ink" iself consisted of a little alum in water. The message was written on ordinary note paper with a pointed stick the size of a pencil. Running a hot iron over what appeared to be a blank sheet of paper caused the message to appear.

While in Vichy, Lily sometimes spent evenings with her friends in the lounge of the Hotel des

Ambassadeurs, curled up in one of the big leather armchairs there, discussing events of the day. Often she nervously scratched the arms of the chair with her long nails. Someone said she looked like a little black cat, which is how Lily got her nickname.

In November 1940, Lily and Roman traveled to Paris to set up their spy network, a difficult and very dangerous mission in the German-occupied city. Paris had been transformed. Red German flags with black swastikas were flying everywhere and there was scarcely any traffic except for German military vehicles. Scowling soldiers walked the streets in their heavy jackboots. Lily was not saddened by what she saw. Instead, she was furious at the people of the city for having surrendered to the Germans without a fight.

Lily went to visit her mother, who was thrilled to see her. When Lily explained why she was in Paris, her mother promised to help her in any way she could.

The next day, Lily found an artist's studio where she and Roman could live and that could serve as their headquarters. Then, with little idea of the risk they were running, they began setting up "Interallié," their spy network. Roman discarded his foreign-sounding name and took on the role of Lily's cousin Armand.

One of their first tasks was recruiting spies, or agents. There were plenty of French men and women ready to work against the Germans, but they had to be instructed in what information was important and how to file their reports. In the case of airfields, for instance, agents had to provide sketches of the runways, taxiways, and hangars. They had to report the number of and type of aircraft, and the location of fuel tanks and ammunition storage areas. They also had to give details about antiaircraft defenses, the types of camouflage in use, and any construction projects that might be underway.

Agents in port cities had to give complete reports on ships arriving and departing, and those at piers or at anchor. Camouflage and port defenses were important, too. Lily and Roman also collected information on the German Army and other military units, communication faclities, fuel storage areas, industrial plants, and electric power stations throughout occupied France.

Lily and Roman worked with amazing success. Their spies watched the movements of German troops and airfields around Paris and in Pas-de-Calais, where bombers took off every night to attack London. They had agents studying the German-controlled French press for news that could be sent to the British. They even had a German-speaking spy reading soldiers' newspapers for tidbits of information.

Getting all the news and information to London was a big problem in the first weeks of operation because Lily and Roman had no radio transmitter with which to send coded messages. Instead, reports from the spy network were photographed. Then, every Wednesday, the microfilm was given to a courier, who boarded the early morning train from Paris to Marseilles in unoccupied southern France. Once the train left the station, the courier went to the bathroom in the dining car and locked the door behind him. He then unscrewed the metal sign that read: *It is forbidden to use the toilet while the train is in the station.* He slipped the microfilm behind the sign, retightened the screws, and left the train at the next station to return to Paris. In Marseilles, another courier picked up the micro-film and the report was transmitted to London.

Early in 1941, the British provided Lily and Ro-man with their own radio transmitter, which sim-plified matters. Regular coded messages began going out from their Paris headquarters that be-gan: "To the War Office, London, for Room XYZ, The Cat reports: . . ."

Sometimes The Cat herself went spying. When information was needed about the sprawling Orly Airfield outside Paris, Lily made a tour of the neighborhoods surrounding the heavily guarded field. On the road opposite the main entrance, she noticed a café with a FOR SALE sign posted in the window. She spoke to the owner, telling him she was interested in the property, and asking him whether she could make a return visit with her architect. "Of course," said the owner.

Lily's "architect" was a fellow spy named Uncle Marco, who was a 50-year-old reservist in the French Army. While Lily chatted with the owner, Uncle Marco sketched the layout of the whole airfield and jotted down the number and types of aircraft in use under the pretense of inspecting the building. Within 24 hours, microfilm copies of Uncle Marco's report were in London.

Another time, the British in London asked Interallié to get intelligence information concerning the Royal Air Force's raid on Brest in northwest France, the site of a huge naval base. London wanted to know how much damage had resulted from the raid.

Lily decided to go and see for herself. By talking to people in the city, Lily was able to get detailed information as to the condition of ships that happened to be in port during the raid, the docks themselves, and the various port facilities. But all her questioning aroused the suspicions of the Nazi Sicherheitsdienst, the German security service. A warning was sent to Paris.

When Lily stepped off the train in Paris the next morning, a Nazi security agent who spoke perfect French was waiting for her. "I am a Gestapo inspector," he said. "Please tell me, Madame, what you were doing in Brest?"

Although she was shaking with fear inside, Lily managed to speak with calm and assurance. "Do you really want to know the truth?" she said, flashing a smile.

"Yes."

"There was so much talk about the R.A.F. raid that, as a curious woman with time on my hands, I wanted to see for myself."

The Gestapo agent stared hard at Lily, then began to laugh. He believed her! But it had been a very close call.

By the fall of 1941, operations of Interallié and other spy networks on the continent of Europe had come under the supervision of Great Britain's Special Operations Executive (SOE), which had been established by Winston Churchill, Britain's wartime leader. SOE officials were eager for a personal meeting with Roman. One night he was picked up by a small, single-engine plane at a secret airfield and flown to London. After a two-week stay, during which time he and the British discussed expanding the Interallié operation, he was parachuted back into occupied France.

On November 16, 1941, Interallié passed its first birthday. It had been a difficult year for Lily. Each day, she and Roman had worked from early morning until late at night, when Lily fell wearily into bed. The hard work was only part of it. Her days and nights were filled with tension and uncertainty. The hazards of spying were beginning to affect her health and sometimes she was depressed. She often thought of how peaceful her former life in North Africa with her husband had been.

Adding to her woes was the knowledge that German radio detection units had been spotted in the streets near their headquarters. The radio transmitter was moved. When the new location proved unsatisfactory, the transmitter was moved again.

There were times that Roman suspected he was

being shadowed. He began to grow uneasy.

Unknown to Lily and Roman and the many agents of Interallié, German military leaders in Paris had begun to realize that a major spy network was at work. Their suspicions had been aroused by the choice of certain targets by British bombers and the timing of the attacks.

Hugo Bleicher, who later was to become an important figure in German counterintelligence, was named to head the investigation. In his mid-forties, tall, and heavily built, Bleicher had been captured by the Allies during World War I. He put his years as a prisoner of war to good use, learning both French and English. When World War II began, Bleicher was called back into the service and assigned to counterintelligence because of his language skills.

Someone tipped off Bleicher that an Interallié courier named Kiki regularly visited the city of Cherbourg. Early in November 1941, Bleicher and one of his officers picked up Kiki at the Cherbourg railroad station.

Back in Paris, Bleicher questioned Kiki. Bleicher did not use the brutal tactics for which the Gestapo would later become well known. Instead, he used a friendly approach, gently persuading prisoners to cooperate. Before long, Bleicher got what he wanted from Kiki: the address of Interallié headquarters.

Bleicher wasted no time in rounding up the members of the spy ring. Early one November morning, German secret police surrounded the building that housed Interallié. When they burst in, they found Roman in his pajamas, sipping coffee. "I am a Polish officer carrying out my duties," Roman announced to the officers who arrested him.

Lily had spent the previous night at a girlfriend's apartment. Returning home around noontime, she noticed her neighborhood seemed much busier than usual. Groups of men with seemingly nothing to do were standing about the street corners. When she reached the doorway of her building, a German soldier went up to her and said, "You've kept us waiting, Madame. Come with me please."

Escorted by two Germans, Lily was taken to a military car parked at the curb. She was very calm.

One of the Germans said, "I suppose you realize why we are here."

"Naturally," Lily replied. "It was a great gamble and today I have lost. But I am a good gambler."

The car pulled away. At a corner near the Interallié headquarters building, it slowed to a stop. On the sidewalk stood Roman's girlfriend, Renée Borni, with a German secret service agent at her side.

She looked at Lily and nodded. "Yes," she said, "that's The Cat."

Lily was taken to the Hotel Edouard VII, which served as the Paris headquarters for the German police, for questioning. Afterward, she was driven to Santé Prison, where she was searched and thrust into a cold, damp, stinking cell.

That night in her prison bed, Lily began to fully

realize all that had happened. Interallié had been destroyed. This was the end.

At eight o'clock the next morning, Lily was brought back to the Hotel Edouard VII. She was taken upstairs and ushered into a private dining room. A waiter served her a delicious breakfast of coffee, cream, freshly baked rolls, and butter.

As she was eating, Hugo Bleicher came into the room. To Lily, he looked tall and massive. "Good morning," he said warmly, and offered Lily a package of cigarettes.

When Lily had finished her breakfast, Bleicher spoke to her kindly, like a friend who wanted to be helpful. "Madame Carré," he said, "we have decided you are far too intelligent and interesting to remain in prison. You know everything and can be of invaluable assistance to me in winding up the Interallié case."

Lily listened without saying a word. Bleicher continued: "You have committed enough crimes to be shot several times over. You have harbored an escaped Polish officer and passed him off as your cousin. You have practiced espionage for more than a year. These are crimes punishable by death, as you well know."

The choice was clear — either work with the Germans or be shot. Lily felt she had no choice but to cooperate with Bleicher and the Nazis and turn her back on her friends.

The German spymaster wanted Lily to begin immediately. He said, "We have read your diary and know that at eleven o'clock on the morning of November nineteenth you are meeting an agent at the Pam Pam bar. You shall keep that appointment and I shall be with you. You shall introduce me as one of your band and when the agent has committed himself, I will arrest him."

On the appointed day, they drove to the Pam Pam. Lily sat at a small table with Bleicher. When the agent arrived, Lily introduced him. After they had chatted for a few minutes, Bleicher offered to drop the agent where he was going. As soon as they were in the car, Bleicher pulled out a pistol, turned to the agent and said, "Well, Monsieur, you are now in a German police car and I am arresting you."

That was Lily's first victim. Next, Bleicher made her call Uncle Marco. She arranged to meet him at Chez Graff at six o'clock that evening. Uncle Marco said he would be bringing André Aubertin, another agent. Bleicher was delighted to be getting two birds with one stone.

When Lily and Bleicher arrived at Chez Graff that evening, he ordered Lily to go in first, while he followed. Lily sat at a small table. Bleicher took a table several feet away. Four German agents were at the bar.

When the unsuspecting Uncle Marco arrived, he kissed Lily on both cheeks and said how good it was to see her. He sat down and immediately began to write a message that he wanted her to send to London. The Germans watched and listened. Then André Aubertin arrived. Hardly had he greeted his friends, when the Germans pounced.

"German police!" one shouted. "Not a word. Follow us."

After long questioning and many beatings, Uncle Marco was sent to the Buchenwald concentration camp. He was later transferred to the Mauthausen camp "for extermination." But Uncle Marco managed to survive the ordeal and later testified against Lily.

One by one, other members of Interallié were arrested by the Germans on the basis of information supplied by Lily. Some were sent to concentration camps but others earned their freedom by agreeing to betray the French, as Lily had done.

One day, Bleicher said to Lily, "We're going to play some fine tricks on the British." Bleicher explained that he planned to have Lily continue sending radio messages to London using one of the Interallié transmitters that had fallen into his hands.

"We will sign the messages 'The Cat,'" said Bleicher. "The British are unaware that we have rounded up Roman and his agents and that you are in our hands."

When Lily's first message went out from Paris, Bleicher was on hand, eager to see how the British would respond. A few minutes after the message had been received in London, the reply came back. "Message received," it said. "Contents agreed." The acceptance of Lily's message meant that Bleicher could now be in day-to-day contact with British intelligence. A bizarre cat-and-mouse game had begun.

A little more than a month after Lily had renewed radio contact with London, she received a
telephone call from a lawyer she knew who asked
if she would be willing to meet "a friend." The
friend turned out to be a British espionage agent
who used the name "Lucas." In his mid-thirties,
intense, and excitable, Lucas had been parachuted
into France several months before to establish a
spy network for the British, but serious problems
had developed. Now Lucas was without money
and out of touch with his London base. The meeting with The Cat had been suggested because it
was known that she was in radio contact with British intelligence in London.

Since Lucas didn't know that Lily had joined the
Germans, he told her everything. He was eager to
return to London to meet with his superiors, he
said. While he had made some progress in setting
up his spy ring, he needed information and advice
from London to get operations moving at full tilt.
He planned to stay in England for only a brief time,
then return to France. Right now he needed
money, and a chance to establish communications
with London so he could arrange his departure.

Lily was delighted by this turn of events. Just as
she had betrayed her French colleagues, now she
was scheming to do the same to the Germans.
Lucas, she realized, could be the means by which
she carried out her plan.

Lily's first step was to go to Bleicher and tell him
about Lucas. Bleicher rubbed his hands in glee as
Lily poured out the story. Of course, once Lucas

returned to France, Bleicher would keep him under close surveillance. When he had his spy ring fully operating, Bleicher would crack down. Bleicher ordered Lily to cooperate with Lucas in every way. "Listen to all he has to say," said Bleicher. "Ask questions. Play up your role in Interallié. Give him everything he needs."

Lily's next move was very risky. She went to Lucas and told him everything — that Interallié no longer existed, that most of its agents were in German prisons, and that she was working for Hugo Bleicher and German intelligence. She told Lucas she wanted to turn her back on the Germans and join forces with him.

Lucas gasped in amazement. His first thought was to shoot Lily. She was, after all, a Germany spy. But he realized that would be stupid, for it would bring a vengeful Bleicher down upon him.

And there was another reason. He had to warn London that The Cat was a double agent and the Interallié radio was a sham. That became his chief goal.

Plans were laid for Lucas to make his journey to England from the Breton coast of France, where he would be picked up by a Royal Navy torpedo boat. A few days before he was scheduled to leave, Lucas had a sudden inspiration: Why not take The Cat with him?

When he told Lily of his plan, she shrugged. "They will not even let me go to Vichy," she said. "What makes you think they will let me go to London?"

"Try to arrange it all the same," Lucas said. "If they agree, I will say in my next message that I am bringing a small-size, lightweight passenger with me, without saying who it is."

"Okay," Lily said. "But it's a dream."

To Lily's astonishment, Bleicher thought the idea to be brilliant. As he saw it, Lily, while in London, would be able to get the names and addresses of countless agents working in France for the Allies, and then return with Lucas. After that, what Bleicher called the "great roundup" would begin.

All of Bleicher's superiors approved the plan, except for an old colonel. "This woman will be your downfall," he told Bleicher.

"I will pay the penalty if she betrays us," Bleicher said. "But I know her intimately and I know she will not."

Lucas and Lily were picked up by the fast British torpedo boat on the night of February 26, 1942. By dawn, they could see the English coast gleaming in the morning sun. They landed at Dartmouth on England's southern coast.

Lucas had hardly stepped ashore when he warned the British of Lily's true role. In the weeks that followed, Lily was questioned for hours on end by British intelligence experts. They were not quite sure what to make of her. Was she really ready to betray the Germans? They could not be certain.

At the end of March, Lucas parachuted back into France. As soon as his presence became known,

Bleicher had him arrested. Lucas spent the rest of the war in the Colditz prisoner-of-war camp.

With Lucas's arrest, there could be no doubt that The Cat was a German spy, and she was imprisoned. In the summer of 1945, with World War II winding down, The Cat was returned to France. She was kept in prison until early in 1949, when she was put on trial.

The prosecuting attorney said of her: "For two months, she practiced the worst kind of treason. Her malice, her cunning, her perseverance in evil, show what she is — a brain without a heart."

Lily admitted her guilt but asked for mercy. "You must admit that this woman was faced with the choice of life or death," said her lawyer. "Do not forget that from the beginning of the resistance she was a heroine. Would you put to death those who at the beginning sowed the seed of faith and later over-estimated their own strength?"

The court decided it would. Lily was sentenced to death. Later the sentence was reduced to life imprisonment and, in 1954, when the strong feelings caused by the war had diminished, Lily was released.

She lived a quiet life in France, out of the public eye, trying to forget her controversial deeds. But when one has lived a life as Lily Carré lived hers, it cannot be easy to forget.

8
Code Name Cynthia

At dawn on November 8, 1942, dozens of snub-nosed landing barges from ships offshore eased onto the sandy beaches just a few miles from Algeria in French North Africa to land hundreds of American troops, artillery, and tanks. Over the city's docks, flames and smoke were still rising from attacks by Allied bombers and shelling by naval guns from the east and west.

Beyond the harbor, well out into the Mediterranean, a great naval task force had been assembled. It included the Royal Navy's battleships *Rodney* and *Nelson*, the aircraft carrier *Argus*, cruisers and destroyers, and transports packed with U.S. troops.

What was happening at Algiers that morning was part of the massive Allied effort to gain control of French North Africa. Called Operation Torch (because it was meant to bring the "torch" of liberty to Algeria, Tunisia, and French Morocco), it involved some 500 troop and supply ships that were escorted by more than 350 warships, plus 400,000 American and British troops, who landed along hundreds of miles of the African coast. It was the biggest amphibious operation in history up to that time.

The landings took the Germans completely by surprise. At many points, Allied troops met practically no opposition as they stormed ashore.

Within two days, the key cities of Algiers and Oran on the Mediterranean, and Casablanca and Rabat on the Atlantic, were in Allied hands. United States forces then pushed eastward across Algeria, while the British advanced into southern Tunisia. By May 1943, following the surrender of hundreds of thousands of Axis troops, all of North Africa was in Allied control.

A spy named Betty Pack, who operated under the code name Cynthia, was one important reason for the quick Allied victory in North Africa. In what was one of the boldest espionage operations of World War II, Pack managed to deliver the enemy's secret code books into the hands of the Allies before the invasion. When American and British forces invaded, Allied military commanders often knew what the enemy was going to do before he did it.

Betty Pack's master stroke has been said to have saved the lives of as many as 100,000 Allied soldiers. It also helped to give the Allies a morale-boosting victory. Until the North African invasion, World War II had been one tragic setback after another for the United States and its partners.

The daughter of a noted Washington lawyer and the husband of a British diplomat, tall and slender Betty Pack was an intelligent and beautiful woman, good at everything she did. She spoke three languages besides English — French, German, and Spanish. These qualities, plus her craving for excitement and danger, helped to make her, as her wartime boss once described her, "the greatest unsung heroine of World War II."

Betty was born Amy Elizabeth Thorpe in Minneapolis on November 22, 1910. She had a sister and brother, both younger. Her father was a Marine Corps colonel, and the family moved about a great deal as his assignments changed. When Betty was ten, the Thorpes settled in Washington, D.C.

Betty's mother believed strongly in good manners and the benefits of being involved in "society." Betty knew early the advantages of privilege and power.

After her father retired from the Marine Corps, he became a lawyer in Washington. Betty, in her teens, attended boarding school at Wellesley (Massachusetts), where she studied music.

Slim and poised, with amber-blond hair and green eyes, Betty, as she approached her twenties, was an adult girl with a mind of her own. She found Washington society "silly and slavish," as she later wrote. She liked older men and dated frequently.

To the surprise of her family and friends, Betty, in 1920, decided to marry Arthur Pack, the Commercial Secretary at the British Embassy. Pack, then 38, was almost twice Betty's age. WASHINGTON DEBUTANTE TO WED BRITISH DIPLOMAT announced a headline on the society page of the *Washington Post*. Six American senators, the attorney general, and countless senior diplomats and foreign ambassadors were among the wedding guests.

Not long after the marriage, Arthur was transferred to Santiago, Chile. His new assignment kept him very busy and Betty was left alone during the day and most evenings. She soon found she had little in common with the wives of the other diplomatic officials, most of whom were much older than she was. She was often bored and lonely.

In 1934, after a daughter had been born to the couple, Arthur was transferred to Spain to take up an assignment at the embassy in Madrid. Betty was thrilled by the idea of living in Europe. But just as in South America, Betty found life as a diplomat's wife rather dull.

A bitter civil war erupted in Spain in 1936. It was to last three years and take the lives of a million Spanish people. Because of the violence in Madrid, the British moved embassy operations to San Sebastian in the north of Spain, just a few miles south of Spain's border with France. Arthur and Betty rented a seaside home in Biarritz, which was on the French side of the border.

One day in a hotel lobby in San Sebastian, Betty

happened to meet five young soldiers, members of the revolutionary force, who had gotten trapped behind enemy lines. They asked Betty to help them get through enemy checkpoints before they were discovered and made captives. Betty sympathized with the men and agreed to aid them. But Arthur said no. Why, he wanted to know, should she risk her life in a fight that was theirs?

Betty paid no attention to Arthur. She loaded the five men into her car and dropped them off beyond the checkpoints. She was not stopped once, thanks to her official diplomat's license plates.

Back home, Betty rejoiced in the fact that she had probably saved the lives of five young men. The experience stirred her up, and she wanted to do more.

It wasn't long before she had another opportunity to put some excitement in her life. In the fall of 1937, Arthur was transferred again, this time to Poland and the Warsaw embassy. It was a tense period in world history. A European war seemed almost certain. In March 1938, Adolf Hitler ordered German troops into Austria and they swiftly conquered the country. Hitler eyed Czechoslovakia as his next victim.

Poland, which shared borders with Germany and Czechoslovakia, was in the center of the storm. At embassy receptions and formal dinners, every conversation focused on the taut political situation. Betty, with her ability to attract and charm highly placed diplomatic officials, was often told what she believed to be important information.

One evening she heard Poland's top-secret military plans for dealing with Hitler. She happened to report what she had been told to Lieutenant Colonel Jack Shelley, the British embassy's passport control officer. The information excited Shelley. He then revealed to Betty that he was also associated with the British Secret Intelligence Service (the SIS or M.I.6) and he asked Betty to get more information of the same type for him.

As Betty continued to provide Shelley with intelligence, he was told by his superiors to recruit her as an agent. Although she had no formal training, Betty seemed to have natural ability for intelligence work. By the spring of 1938, Betty was working as an agent for the British Secret Intelligence Service.

Betty's instructions were simple: Make friends with men in high positions in the Polish government and entice them into giving her information. She was told to do more entertaining so as to widen her circle of contacts. Betty loved the idea of being a British agent. The work was a constant challenge. No longer was she the least bit bored.

From one government official, Betty learned that Polish mathematicians had begun to crack the previously unbreakable code written by the German machine known as Enigma. This intelligence was later to pay rich dividends in British efforts to crack the Enigma codes. In 1938, on a mission to Prague in Czechoslovakia, Betty was successful in obtaining German plans for an invasion of that country.

That was Betty's last espionage success for a number of years. Arthur was forced to give up his diplomatic post in Warsaw because of illness. When he was later able to work, he was assigned to Santiago, Chile, once again. Betty missed the excitement and danger of being a secret agent. There was little to spy on in Chile. Her great boredom was surely one reason she decided to separate from her husband. In 1941, Betty returned to the United States to begin a new life. Arthur and their daughter remained in Chile.

Betty did not have to wait long before starting to work as an agent again. When she arrived in New York, she was handed a letter addressed to her mother from one "J. Howard." He explained in the letter that he was sorry to have missed Betty when he called to see her. The letter contained a New York telephone number that Betty was to use to get in touch with Mr. Howard. From her experience with British intelligence, Betty knew the name "John Howard" was one often used as a cover by agents.

When she called the number and spoke to "John Howard," he sounded pleased to hear from her. His real name was John Pepper, the man explained, and he was a senior aide with British Secret Intelligence in the Western Hemisphere, an operation that had its headquarters in New York and was headed by William Stephenson. Also known as "A Man Called Intrepid" through a book and Hollywood film of that name, Stephenson was also referred to as "The Chief," and "Little Bill."

Stephenson wanted Betty to work among the foreign diplomats who were based in Washington. He especially wanted her to penetrate the German and Italian embassy staffs. Betty was given the code name "Cynthia" and instructed to rent a house in Washington. Her expenses would be paid by the British and she would receive a salary of several hundred dollars a month.

Betty's first target was the Italian embassy. (On June 11, 1940, Italy had entered World War II on the side of Germany.) It did not take Betty long to develop a close relationship with an admiral who was chief of military intelligence at the embassy. She told him that she had a friend at ONI (the Office of Naval Intelligence) who badly wanted the Italian naval ciphers. Similar to a code, a cipher is a form of secret communication that rearranges letters or uses substitutes for them in disguising a message.

The ciphers would enable the Americans and British to read Italy's secret messages. Betty told the admiral that by getting her the ciphers he would be helping both America and Italy at the same time.

The admiral explained he couldn't provide the ciphers himself, but he gave her the name of an embassy code clerk, desperately in need of money, who would be willing to sell them. The details were quickly arranged and the ciphers came into Allied hands.

The timing couldn't have been better. Units of the British Navy in the Mediterranan were about to be challenged by the Italian fleet. The chief goal of the Italians was to attack British ships sailing from Africa to Greece. But in a sea battle near Cape Matapan off the southern tip of Greece late in March 1941, British ships, although greatly outnumbered, were able to destroy an important part of the Italian Navy.

The Royal Navy's victory may have resulted from the fact that British intelligence was in possession of the Italian Navy's cipher. The British commander in chief was able to know enemy strategy in advance and act accordingly.

Following Betty's success with the Italians, she was next asked to focus on the Vichy French. After the armies of Adolf Hitler had forced the French to surrender in June 1940, the Germans divided France into two zones, one occupied by their troops. The other, in southern France, was unoccupied. In the unoccupied zone, a government was established at Vichy.

The Vichy government controlled French possessions in North Africa which, in the early stages of World War II, had come to have critical importance. During the early months of 1942, the Allies began to plan an invasion of North Africa. Besides forcing the Germans and Italians out of Africa, the invasion would give the German high command something else to worry about, thereby helping to relieve pressure on hard-pressed Russian forces, which were under German attack along a 2,000 mile front that extended from the Arctic to the Baltic Sea.

Both the British and Americans were uneasy about the Vichy French. The head of the Vichy government was Marshal Henri Pétain, an 80-year old French military hero. But everyone realized that Pétain was a mere figurehead. The real power was Admiral Jean Darlan, an open admirer of the Nazis.

Betty was asked to find out all she could about the ambassador and other key people at the Vichy embassy in Washington. Her method was direct. She called Charles Brousse, the embassy's director of press relations, told him she was a journalist who supported the Vichy government, and asked whether she could interview the ambassador.

Betty's request was granted and the interview went well. She had achieved her first objective.

Betty felt that she would be hearing from Brousse again, and she was right. In the weeks that followed their first meeting, she and Brousse met many times and became romantically involved. Betty had hoped Brousse would be attracted to her, and he was. However, she hadn't figured on falling in love with him. Their relationship was to last for more than twenty years.

One day, not long after they had first met, Betty told Charles she had a "confession" to make to him. She then explained that she was working for British intelligence and wanted to get information about Britain's enemies or potential enemies out of the embassy. She wanted to know whether

Charles would be willing to help her.

Charles said he would. At that stage, he couldn't deny Betty anything. So it was that in July 1941, Charles began providing intelligence to Betty on a daily basis.

Charles realized, of course, that he was putting himself at enormous risk. He constantly reminded Betty that, if his role was revealed, his career would be ruined. That was not the worst of it. He had no doubt that, were he to be exposed, the Vichy secret police would deal out their own brand of justice, and would probably have him killed.

The information Betty obtained each day from Charles was speedily transmitted to British intelligence in New York. Little of importance happened at the embassy that the British did not find out about.

On December 7, 1941, the Japanese bombed Pearl Harbor. The attack killed or wounded about 3,700 persons and dealt the Pacific Fleet a crippling blow. The next day, President Franklin Roosevelt asked Congress for a declaration of war. Only one member of Congress voted against the declaration. On December 11, Congress declared war against Germany and Italy. With America's entry into the war, Betty began working for the Office of Strategic Services (OSS), a forerunner of the Central Intelligence Agency, as well as for British intelligence.

Allied leaders wondered how America's participation in the war was going to affect the Vichy French. They were especially worried about the

French fleet in the Mediterranean. They wanted to know how the French were planning to use those ships and whether there was any chance they might be seized by the Germans. Overnight, the intelligence being gathered by Betty had taken on much greater importance.

One day Betty received a message from John Pepper, her intelligence contact in New York, who told her he had an important matter to discuss with her. In a New York hotel room, Pepper explained that British intelligence in London had asked whether Betty could get the naval code used by the Vichy French. The request, Pepper said, came "from the top."

The code was contained in closely guarded cipher books. If British codebreakers could get a look at the books, they would be able to read all the messages being transmitted by the Vichy French and thereby get some insight into their plans. And with the Allies planning an invasion of Vichy territory in North Africa, the code books could be invaluable.

When Betty returned to Washington and told Charles what she needed, he was shocked. He tried to discourage her, pointing out that the cipher books were closely guarded day and night. Getting to them would be an impossible task, he said.

During daytime hours, only cipher clerks and senior officials were allowed in the code room, Charles explained. The clerks decoded incoming messages and encoded outgoing ones. The ambassador, the head of naval intelligence, and the official who handed messages to the cipher officer were the only other people allowed in the code room. Even Charles himself was barred from entering.

At night, the naval cipher, contained in two thick volumes, each the size of a library-size dictionary, was locked in a safe in the naval intelligence office. The room itself was padlocked.

The embassy was patrolled by an armed watchman with a trained guard dog. In addition, the Vichy secret police had to be considered. Charles said they, too, might play a role in guarding the embassy.

Betty admitted that getting the cipher books was not going to be easy, but it was not impossible. In the weeks that followed, she could hardly think of anything else.

Eventually, Betty, with the help of Charles, devised an elaborate plan. She and Charles would enter the embassy late at night. Charles would use his own key or the guard, with whom Charles had become friendly, would admit them. Once inside, they would unlock a window allowing a safecracker, who was to be provided by British intelligence, to enter. The safecracker would figure out the combination of the safe and remove the code books. He would then hurry with the code books to a room in the nearby Wardman Park Hotel that had been set up as a photo studio. The books would be photographed page by page, then returned to Betty and Charles and put back in the safe. It all had to be done before dawn, when the embassy security staff arrived for the day.

June 23, 1942, was set as the date to execute the plan. Shortly after midnight, Betty and Charles left the Wardman Park Hotel and walked to the embassy. Charles opened the front door with his key. The watchman and his dog were nowhere to be seen. Perhaps he is making his rounds, thought Betty. Charles figured the man was probably dozing.

Betty and Charles first went to the embassy's reception room, where they sat on a couch and talked softly in the darkness. When they heard the guard coming to investigate, they quickly embraced. The guard entered the room and Betty and Charles were caught in the beam of his powerful flashlight. As soon as he saw the two of them together on the couch, the embarrassed guard apologized for interrupting, switched off the flashlight, and left.

Betty had been instructed how to remove the lock from the door of the naval intelligence office, and as soon as the guard had gone, she did so. Inside the room, she opened a window looking out onto a courtyard. The safecracker was already there, ready to mount a ladder he had propped up against the side of the building.

On a signal from Betty, the safecracker ascended the ladder, climbed through the window, and went to work on the safe. Within minutes, he swung open the safe door, reached in, and removed the books. Betty couldn't resist flipping through the pages before handing them back to the safecracker who climbed out of the window and down the ladder with them. A car was waiting to whisk him to the Wardman Park Hotel where the books would be photographed.

Betty closed the safe and replaced the lock on the office door. Then she and Charles went back to the reception room to wait. It was shortly after 1 A.M. From time to time, Betty would reenter the office to see if the safecracker had returned. Time passed slowly. Betty and Charles strained their ears for the slightest sound that would indicate their tense wait was over. Neither one could even think of sleeping.

The deadline was 4 A.M. Even if all the copying was not completed by that time, it was agreed that the safecracker was to return with the cipher books. At 3:55, Betty went to the window and looked out. There was no sign of anyone. The deadline came and went, and still the safecracker did not appear.

As the minutes passed, Betty and Charles became deeply worried. Something must have gone wrong. They smoked cigarettes and paced nervously.

Finally, at 4:40 A.M., Betty saw the safecracker in the yard below. She gasped a sigh of relief as he mounted the ladder. He handed the precious books through the window to her, then climbed into the room and locked them in the safe. After the safecracker had left, Betty removed any trace of fingerprints and closed and locked the office door.

114

It was 5 A.M. when Betty and Charles left the embassy. Both were in high spirits, knowing they had done exactly what they had set out to do.

They went directly to the Wardman Park Hotel and the room that had served as a photo studio. It was filled with cameras on tripods, lights, and technicians. And spread out to dry on the floor, tables, and other pieces of furniture were photographic prints of the pages from the cipher books.

That same day, the copies of the pages were sent to British intelligence in London. All messages to and from the Vichy embassy could now be read by the Allies. It was as if the Allies had been given a window on French North Africa and Nazi-controlled Europe as well. Several months later, in November 1942, when the Allies launched Operation Torch, the invasion of French North Africa, American and British military leaders were able to read the enemy's coded messages. This helped the Allies to carry out the landings with as little fighting as possible.

Betty's spectacular success at the Vichy embassy marked the peak of her career. Other assignments were discussed but never carried out. Betty didn't seem to mind the absence of excitement in her life, for she had fallen deeply in love with Charles Brousse. After Betty divorced Arthur Pack, she and Charles were married.

In 1945, the same year that World War II ended, Betty saw an old French château that resembled a castle in the Pyrenees Mountains about 20 miles from the Spanish border, and fell in love with it.

Charles bought the castle for her and spent a small fortune making it liveable. She and Charles lived there happily for years.

Betty spent much of her leisure time writing letters and keeping in touch with her many friends throughout the world. She also worked with a biographer on a book and a series of newspaper articles that told of her exploits as a British and American espionage agent. The book, titled *Cynthia*, was published in 1966 (three years after Betty's death). It accurately portrayed Betty as a charming and entertaining woman, brave and smart, who enjoyed life, and whose courage and determination during a time of crisis helped to change the course of World War II.

For Further Reading

Axelrod, Alan. *The War Between the Spies*, New York: Atlantic Monthly Press, 1992.

Bakeless, John. *Turncoats, Traitors and Heroes.* Philadelphia, J.B. Lippincott, 1959.

Barton, George. *The World's Greatest Military Spies*. Boston: Page Co., 1917.

Carré, Mathilde-Lily. *I Was the Cat*. London: Souvenir Press, 1960.

Dulles, Allen. *Great True Spy Stories*. New York: Harper & Row, 1968.

Franklin, Charles. *The Great Spies*, New York: Hart Publishing Co., 1967.

Hall, Richard. *Patriots in Disguise, Women Warriors of the Civil War*. New York, Paragon House, 1993.

Hoeling, A.A. *Women Who Spied*. New York: Dodd, Mead, 1967.

Horan, James. D. *Desperate Women*. New York: Putnam's, 1950.

Kahn, David. *The Codebreakers*. New York: Macmillan, 1968.

Komroff, Manuel. *True Adventures of Spies*. Boston: Little Brown, 1954.

Lovell, Mary S. *Cast No Shadow. The Life of the American Spy Who Changed the Course of World War II* [Betty Pack]. New York, Pantheon Books, 1992.

MacDonald, Elizabeth P. *Undercover Girl*. New York: Macmillan, 1947.

Prange, Gordon W. *At Dawn We Slept, The Untold Story of Pearl Harbor*. New York: McGraw-Hill, 1981.

Ranelagh, John. *The Agency: The Rise and Decline of the CIA*. New York: Simon & Schuster, 1986.

Ross, Ishbel. *Rebel Rose*. New York: Harper, 1994.

Singer, Kurt. *Spies and Traitors of World War II*. New York, Prentice Hall, 1945.

Singer, Kurt. *The World's Thirty Greatest Women Spies*. New York: Wilfred Funk, 1951.

Stern, Philip Van Doren. *Secret Mission of the Civil War*. New York: Bonanza Books, 1990.

Stevenson, William. *A Man Called Intrepid*. New York: Harcourt Brace Jovanovich, 1976.

Tully, Andrew. *The Super Spies*. New York: Morrow, 1969.

Volkman, Ernest. *Spies, The Secret Agents Who Changed the Course of History*. New York: John Wiley & Sons, 1994.

Picture Credits

Pictures 1–1, 1–2, 2–1, 8–2: Library of Congress. **Picture 2–2:** Alberti/Lowe Collection. **Pictures 3–1, 3–2:** State Archives of Michigan. **Pictures 4–1, 6–1, 7–1:** AP/Wide World. **Picture 4–2:** U.S. Navy. **Pictures 5–1, 6–2:** National Archives. **Picture 7–2:** from *I Was the Cat*, by Lily Belard, published by Éditions Morgan, 1960. **Picture 8–1:** Washington *Star* collection, Martin Luther King Memorial Library, Washington, D.C.

SCHOLASTIC BIOGRAPHY

☐ MP45877-9	Ann M. Martin: The Story of the Author of The Baby-sitters Club	$3.50
☐ MP44075-6	Bo Jackson: Playing the Games	$2.95
☐ MP44767-X	The First Woman Doctor	$3.50
☐ MP43628-7	Freedom Train: The Story of Harriet Tubman	$2.95
☐ MP42402-5	Harry Houdini: Master of Magic	$2.99
☐ MP42404-1	Helen Keller	$2.99
☐ MP44652-5	Helen Keller's Teacher	$2.95
☐ MP44818-8	Invincible Louisa	$3.50
☐ MP42395-9	Jesse Jackson: A Biography	$3.25
☐ MP43503-5	Jim Abbott: Against All Odds	$2.99
☐ MP41344-9	John F. Kennedy: America's 35th President	$3.25
☐ MP41159-4	Lost Star: The Story of Amelia Earhart	$3.50
☐ MP44350-X	Louis Braille, The Boy Who Invented Books for the Blind	$2.99
☐ MP46050-1	Magic: The Earvin Johnson Story	$2.95
☐ MP48109-6	Malcolm X: By Any Means Necessary	$3.95
☐ MP65174-9	Michael Jordan	$3.50
☐ MP44154-X	Nelson Mandela "No Easy Walk to Freedom"	$3.50
☐ MP42897-7	One More River to Cross: The Stories of Twelve Black Americans	$3.50
☐ MP46572-4	Our 42nd President: Bill Clinton	$2.95
☐ MP43052-1	The Secret Soldier: The Story of Deborah Sampson	$2.99
☐ MP47785-4	Shaquille O'Neal	$2.95
☐ MP42560-9	Stealing Home: A Story of Jackie Robinson	$3.25
☐ MP42403-3	The Story of Thomas Alva Edison, Inventor: The Wizard of Menlo Park	$2.75
☐ MP44212-0	Wanted Dead or Alive: The True Story of Harriet Tubman	$3.95
☐ MP42904-3	The Wright Brothers at Kitty Hawk	$2.95

Available wherever you buy books, or use this order form.

Scholastic Inc., P.O. Box 7502, 2931 East McCarty Street, Jefferson City, MO 65102

Please send me the books I have checked above. I am enclosing $_____ (please add $2.00 to cover shipping and handling). Send check or money order — no cash or C.O.D.s please.

Name_____ Birthdate _____

Address_____

City_____ State/Zip _____

Please allow four to six weeks for delivery. Available in the U.S. only. Sorry, mail orders are not available to residents of Canada. Prices subject to change.

BIO695